## ABOUT THE AUTHOR

Agnes Ravatn is a Norwegian author and columnist. She made her literary début with the novel *Week 53* in 2007. Since then she has written a number of critically acclaimed and award-winning essay collections, including *Standing*, *Popular Reading* and *Operation Self-discipline*, in which she recounts her experience with social-media addiction, and how she overcame it.

Her debut thriller, *The Bird Tribunal*, won the cultural radio P2's listener's prize in addition to The Youth's Critic's Prize, and was made into a successful play, which premiered in Oslo in 2015. The English translation, published by Orenda Books in 2016, was a WHSmith Fresh Talent Pick, winner of a PEN Translation Award, a BBC Radio Four 'Book at Bedtime' and shortlisted for the Dublin Literary Award and the 2017 Petrona Award for Best Scandinavian Crime Novel of the Year.

## ABOUT THE TRANSLATOR

Rosie Hedger was born in Scotland and completed her MA (Hons) in Scandinavian Studies at the University of Edinburgh. She has lived and worked in Norway, Sweden and Denmark, and now lives in York where she works as a freelance translator. Rosie translated Agnes Ravatn's *The Bird Tribunal* for Orenda Books and her translation of Gine Cornelia Pedersen's *Zero* was shortlisted for the Oxford-Weidenfeld Translation Prize 2019. Follow Rosie on Twitter @rosie_hedger.

# The Seven Doors

Agnes Ravatn

Translated from the Norwegian by Rosie Hedger

**ORENDA**
**BOOKS**

O
16
W

London
www.orendabooks.co.uk

First published in Norwegian as *Dei sju dørene* by Samlaget in 2019
First published in English by Orenda Books in 2020
Copyright © Agnes Ravatn, 2019
English translation copyright © Rosie Hedger, 2020

Agnes Ravatn has asserted her moral right to be identified as the author of this work in accordance with the Copyright, Designs and Patents Act, 1988.

A catalogue record for this book is available from the British Library.
ISBN 978-1-913193-38-6
eISBN 978-1-913193-39-3

This book has been translated with financial support from NORLA

**N NORLA**
NORWEGIAN LITERATURE ABROAD

Typeset in Garamond by typesetter.org.uk

Printed and bound by CPI Group (UK) Ltd, Croydon CR0 4YY

# Sunday 18<sup>th</sup> November

Berg slinks along the walls, just as the two surveyors did the week before. Nina pours coffee into the pot and finds a bowl for the dark chocolate.

Yes, Berg says eventually, her voice silky-smooth, then click-clacks her way over to join Nina. It'll set them back a pretty penny, this place.

She is wearing a tight-fitting black suit and a cream blouse. Even in high heels, Nina towers over her.

I'd have preferred to keep the house, all the same, Nina replies, sounding more sombre than she expected to.

I can understand that, Berg replies. How long have you lived here?

It's my childhood home, Nina says, placing another log on the fire. We moved back in when my daughter was born. That was thirty-five years ago now.

So many memories... Berg says, head cocked to one side reassuringly, and Nina's genuine sorrow at losing the house, the acute mournfulness with which it fills her, gives way to irritation at Berg's apparent inability to complete a sentence.

She glances at the clock.

He'll be here soon, she says, but Berg waves a dismissive hand, as if suggesting Nina should relax. Nina plucks a few withered leaves from the pot plants along the windowsill as she gazes outside.

This is certainly an unusual case, the lawyer says, and Nina turns around.

A member of the city council being called upon to demolish his own house, I mean.

Mads was obviously prohibited from having any say in the case, Nina replies, but yes.

They hear the front door open, and moments later he comes galloping up the stairs with Milja riding on his back. He comes to an abrupt halt when he catches sight of the lawyer.

Oh, hello, he says, clearing his throat. He slides Milja down onto the floor and offers the lawyer an outstretched hand.

Mads Glaser, he says. It's very good of you to come out here on a Sunday.

I've been to Gingerbread Land, Milja declares proudly. Her plump cheeks are bright red. Berg offers her an ingratiating smile.

Yes, our granddaughter is spending the day with us, Nina says. But I'm sure a bit of television will keep her busy for a little while. She nods at Mads, who ushers Milja into the next room.

Nina and Berg each pull out a chair at the dining table. Mads pulls off his woolly jumper and smooths his shirt before joining them. His grey-black hair curls by his ears.

Berg extracts a thick wad of documents from her bag and perches a pair of spectacles at the end of her nose, spectacles that Nina suspects are just for show.

Berg's well-manicured mother-of-pearl nails leaf through various sheets of paper before she pauses to look up at them.

A brief introduction to the legal aspects of compulsory acquisition, perhaps?

Yes, please— Nina begins, but Mads interrupts her.

No, he says, that won't be necessary. As I explained on the phone, we're prepared to accept a reasonable settlement.

OK? Berg says, looking at Nina, who nods reluctantly.

Berg begins outlining matters, moving rather rapidly as she walks Nina and Mads through their rights now that a final decision has been made about the proposed light-rail route, which is set to split their living room in two.

Nina listens, her brow furrowed, trying to look like she is following what's being said in spite of the onslaught of legal jargon that involves. She exchanges discreet glances with Mads, who rolls his eyes before getting up.

Coffee? he says, cutting Berg off mid-flow. He picks up the coffee pot and pours her a cup, standing to her left, as if he were a waiter.

We can also ask that the council covers any costs incurred by the move, Berg continues. We can even demand that they pay for things like new curtains, for instance, if the old ones won't fit in the new house. It all depends just how far they're willing to go.

Not all that far, I should think, wouldn't you say? Mads says, scratching his temple.

Will we receive any help to find somewhere else? Nina asks, or will we simply receive a sum of money and have to find something by ourselves?

Berg laughs initially, as if the question has been asked in jest, but quickly realises that Nina is being sincere.

You'll have to find something by yourselves, yes, she replies with a quiet cough. And I'd start looking now, if I were you.

Good God, we'll spend every weekend for the foreseeable future traipsing around viewings and worrying about who's bidding what, Nina says to Mads, clearly less than delighted by the news.

It's a toss-up between Haukeland and Nygårdshøyden, then, Mads says. Rock, paper, scissors, come on, he says, raising a fist in Nina's direction. Which of us will be rewarded with the shortest commute?

You won't be standing for re-election, then? Berg asks.

He shrugs.

I never thought I'd hear myself say it, but I've started to miss all those blocked sinuses. When it comes to *actually* making a difference in people's lives, working in the ear, nose and throat department beats the local council, hands down.

Oh dear, the lament of the long-suffering health-board representative, Nina says. But which of us has the most years left to work? I'll only be attending viewings within a hundred-metre radius of the faculty of humanities.

Well, it's just a case of starting to look, even if the demolition itself is some way off. As you know, Berg adds, looking at Mads, I think we can secure a fair settlement if we make it clear that we're willing to act quickly.

Nina is hit with a wave of nausea when she hears the word 'demolition'; she brings her napkin to her mouth and coughs quietly.

And looking at this house, I might even go so far as to say that the challenge will be finding something of a sufficiently high standard, Berg says. If you're hoping for something equal in terms of condition and style, that is.

Hear, hear, Mads replies.

That's if you don't take the most straightforward route and simply move into the house on Birkeveien, the lawyer says.

Mads looks at Nina inquiringly, who in turn looks at Berg.

You could avoid house-hunting entirely, then simply invest the money you receive, she says.

Out of the question, Nina says firmly. A renovation project from, gosh, when were they built?

The 1950s, at the latest, Mads says. No, that's not an option we're prepared to consider.

Berg removes her spectacles. She brings the palms of her hands together with her fingertips touching as if she were some kind of criminal mastermind, resting her elbows on the table as she leans towards her clients.

Very well. In that case, shall we devise a plan that ensures the best possible result? she asks, and Nina nods bravely.

They stand at the living-room window and watch the black Audi, which Berg manoeuvres back and forth at a snail's pace for at least a minute before finally managing to turn it around.

It's so surreal, the whole thing, Nina sighs as the car slips down the hill in the dusky light of early afternoon. She catches sight of her own reflection, her eyes two dark spheres, the rain trickling down.

You're not wrong there, he says, his hand stroking her dark, shoulder-length hair.

Is it just me, or have you been wearing black more often than usual these days? he asks, carefully plucking a hair from her dress.

This is my first major life crisis, she replies. I need to mark that somehow.

He steps back and takes a seat at the piano stool. He places his fingers gently on the keys and begins to play Couperin's 'Les Barricades Mystérieuses' at a slow tempo.

*Stop it!* a voice shouts from the television room.

Thirty-five years, Nina says. Don't you feel even a little sentimental about it all?

He smiles despondently.

I've done all that I can do, he says, his eyes on the sheet music. It wasn't to be.

I know, she sighs.

Now we just have to make the best of things. And secure a respectable settlement, at the very least.

She stands in silence, gazing out at the allotment over the road. She'll miss it in the springtime. She pulls out a chair and takes a seat.

Birkeveien, she says suddenly, turning to face him. Who's renting it at the moment?

A young single mother, he replies without lifting his fingers from the keys. She's been there for a few years now.

Do you think we ought to sell that place too?

What makes you say that? he asks.

I don't know, she says with a shrug. For simplicity's sake.

It might be a nice option for Ingeborg and the family in due course, he says.

So my childhood home doesn't matter but your aunt's old place...

He lifts his hands from the piano and rubs his palms against his trouser legs. Looks at her.

I know, she says. I know. You did everything you could.

Jo reckons renting the place out is a good idea.

Oh, Jo, the housing-market expert, she replies sardonically.

She walks over and sits down at the dining-room table, taking a few crackers and some cheese and fruit and placing them on a plate.

Strange, she says. I don't remember Aunt Lena's funeral.

Not that strange, really, given that you weren't there.

I wasn't?

She died when you went on that field trip to Copenhagen.

Milja bounds into the room and clambers up onto her grandad's lap. It's Pippi Longstocking, Mads sings, and pretends to play an accordion as Milja slams the piano keys at random.

What time did we say we'd drop off this little tyke? he asks.

As Ingeborg makes her way downstairs, Milja is holding Mads' hand and gazing, bewitched, at one of the prehistoric-looking crocodiles. The reptile stands behind the thick glass, stock still in the water, and returns Milja's stare with a stiff, vacant expression.

Mummy! Milja cries with delight, letting go of her grandad's hand. Ingeborg crouches down and accepts her bounding embrace.

Mummy, I saw a shark, Milja says with a grave expression, and Ingeborg raises her eyebrows appreciatively.

Grandad will take you to see the monkeys, she says, standing up and sending her father a meaningful look. Grandma and I are just going to have a little chat in the café.

Mads looks at Nina quizzically as she is ushered upstairs by their daughter, she shrugs in response with a puzzled look on her face.

They take a seat at the table in the furthest corner of the half-empty café.

Ingeborg drapes her grey wool coat over the back of her chair but keeps her scarf on. She's wrapped it around her neck in some sort of intricate fashion.

Nina pulls out her purse and stands up.

What do you fancy?

Golden milk, Ingeborg replies.

Pardon me?

Ingeborg looks at her mother with resignation.

Soya milk with turmeric? she says.

Ingeborg, it's a hot-dog stand. You'll be lucky to get a cup of tea.

Ice water, then.

Funny old things, daughters, Nina thinks to herself as she queues to pay. She glances discreetly over at Ingeborg, who is entirely absorbed by her mobile phone as penguins waddle around in the background.

She ponders the Electra complex, the female version of the Oedipus complex proposed by Carl Jung, young daughters fantasising about killing their mothers in order to fully possess their fathers. Freud never acknowledged the Electra complex as a genuine phenomenon, but she's thought about it on numerous occasions and wondered if Jung might have been on to something.

So, what was it you wanted to talk to me about? Nina asks gently once she's returned to the table.

Ingeborg opens her mouth to reply, but her face falls and she breaks down before she manages to utter a word.

Nina furrows her brow as her daughter struggles to compose herself and assume a normal expression once again.

It's only now that she notices the dark circles under her daughter's eyes. Her hair has been scraped into a chaotic bun at the nape of her neck, and her shoulders are high and pointed, razor-sharp.

We've got silverfish, she says eventually, her voice thick with emotion.

Silverfish? Nina repeats, doing her best not to laugh. My God, I thought you were ill!

Ingeborg stares at her mother in disbelief.

We've been up all night, she says. Eirik is hysterical.

But they're not doing you any harm, are they?

There are people at the house as I speak, Ingeborg says, resigned. We managed to find a company willing to come out at the weekend.

Everyone gets bugs of some sort every once in a while.

*Silverfish!* her daughter repeats shrilly.

So that was why we had Milja today, Nina replies cheerfully. You were on the hunt for creepy-crawlies.

We'll have to sell up, Ingeborg whispers, furtively glancing around the room.

Surely it's the sort of thing you'd be obliged to inform any buyer about? Nina begins, but she is quickly hushed.

We need something bigger anyway, Ingeborg says. She rests her head in her hands and massages her temples.

The whole lot of us will be homeless before too long, Nina says.

We're a room short, Ingeborg says, glancing up at her mother.

Is that right?

Hint, hint, Ingeborg says.

Hint, hint?

Ingeborg sighs loudly.

You might be a professor of literature, but you're incapable of reading between the lines, it seems.

Nina gazes at her daughter in disbelief before finally putting two and two together.

Six weeks, Ingeborg says. I'm exhausted.

But Ingeborg! Nina says, hugging her daughter across the table. That's fantastic!

Thanks, her daughter says feebly, looking up at her mother with tired eyes.

We have to tell your father, Nina says, craning her neck to see if she can see him outside.

I thought we might wait a bit, Ingeborg says. I wanted to see if you might be able to … talk him round a bit.

About what, exactly?

An advance on our inheritance, Ingeborg mouths, almost without uttering a sound.

Listen, Nina says, patting her hand gently. Do you remember Aunt Lena?

# Monday 19th November

Towards the end of the day she receives a message from Ingeborg. She's clocking off at 3pm, she writes. Could they take a look at the house on Birkeveien before picking Milja up from nursery?

She glances outside. It's dry for once, the sun low in the sky. A stroll would do her good.

She hasn't been there for years, she can't remember the house number. She calls Mads, but there's no answer. She searches the street name in her email inbox and finds an email between Mads and their financial advisor she was copied into four years ago. Birkeveien 61.

She pulls up a map on her phone and vaguely remembers visiting Aunt Lena many years ago now, an attractive Bergen lady with a walking frame who lived in a house filled with steep staircases.

Ingeborg is waiting for her outside the hospital building, tall and slim. She waves cheerfully when she catches sight of her mum and walks over to meet her just as an air ambulance lands on the helipad behind her.

How are you doing? Nina asks, but her daughter bats the question away, excited at the prospect of a terraced house in Landås.

Nina had been surprised when Ingeborg chose to pursue medicine like her father; she hadn't ever felt that her daughter belonged in a job that called for warmth and empathy. All the same, she was pleased that her daughter had chosen such a practical career. What is the point in all of this? she had often wondered as she had watched her own students graduate, only to drift around in ambiguous professions within the culture and education sectors for unforeseeable periods of time.

With the help of the map on her phone, Nina leads the way

along Idrettsveien and Gimleveien, past Brann Stadium, until they eventually reach Birkeveien. They pass two nursery schools and one supermarket en route. There's something uncomfortably earnest about Ingeborg's manner, she's prowling like a cat, rosy-cheeked, airing every thought that enters her head for all to hear.

Cynical children, Nina thinks to herself, it must be my punishment; I must have been doing something wrong during all my years of parenting. But what?

Here we are, Nina says eventually, stopping in her tracks. She looks from the phone to the house number. Ingeborg lets out a gasp.

And what a house it is too, she whispers.

They're standing outside a small, ochre-yellow, semi-detached house over three floors, with red roof tiles and a front garden concealed behind a beech hedge, dense with crisp brown leaves.

Fourteen minutes and twenty-seven seconds, Ingeborg says excitedly, looking up from her watch. And with two nurseries along the way. Mum...

She looks at her mother pleadingly.

It's ideal, certainly, Nina says.

And I do love the colour, Ingeborg says, her gaze fixed lovingly on the yellow façade.

First, we need to speak to your father, Nina says, lifting a hand to curtail Ingeborg's excitement.

Ingeborg is already halfway through the gate, and Nina realises that it's pointless to try to stop her.

A woman's bicycle with a child's seat on the back has been left leaning against the wall beside the front door. There's no sign of a nameplate. The gravel crunches underfoot as if they were wearing horseshoes; Ingeborg scuttles over to the corner of the property to get an idea of what the back garden looks like.

It's certainly very nice, she says loudly, seeking her mother's endorsement.

It's family-friendly, in any case, Nina says, bringing a finger to her lips to hush her daughter's loud excitement.

There's a light on upstairs, Ingeborg says, and before Nina can stop her, she's pressed the doorbell.

But Ingeborg... she says.

What? Ingeborg says, looking somewhat aggressive.

Someone lives here.

Well yes. In our house.

She must be at work, Nina says. It's only quarter past three.

But I heard something.

I didn't hear anything, Nina says.

They stand there for a few moments. Nina can tell from the frosty mist surrounding Ingeborg that she is breathing quickly.

We can hardly go barging in unannounced, she says.

Ingeborg leans forwards and presses the doorbell again, holding it for an extra-long time. Nina turns to walk back out onto the street, distancing herself from Ingeborg's persistence.

We'll call or write, she says. Then we'll come back in a few days' time. There's no great rush, after all.

Her daughter gazes at her beseechingly.

Eirik booked an agent this morning. We're putting our place on the market as soon as we can, do you know how quickly a colony of silverfish multiplies?

In that same instant, someone tentatively opens the front door.

Ingeborg spins around on the gravel.

A young woman gazes back through the gap in the door. Behind her is a serious-looking little boy, dark-eyed and dark-haired, just like his mother.

I've seen you before, Nina thinks to herself as she locks eyes with the woman, but she can't quite place her.

The woman looks at her unanticipated guests expectantly.

Peekaboo! Ingeborg says, an excited expression on her face as she peers at the boy, who clings to his mother's burgundy wool jumper.

The woman looks from Ingeborg to Nina and back to Ingeborg again.

Yes? she says.

Ingeborg Wisløff Glaser, she says. We're the owners of the property.

Ingeborg, Nina whispers.

The woman at the door furrows her brow.

This is my mother, Ingeborg says, nodding in Nina's direction as her mother takes a step back.

Hi there, she says in as friendly a tone as she can muster. It wasn't our intention to disturb you, she begins, but she is interrupted by Ingeborg.

Could we have a little look around the house? she asks.

The woman looks at Ingeborg with a puzzled expression.

Oh, Ingeborg says, turning to her mother. She doesn't speak Norwegian. *Excuse us*, Ingeborg enunciates emphatically, starting again, *we are the landlords*.

Yes, the woman says, I understand what you're saying.

Ingeborg, this is starting to sound like a raid, Nina says under her breath.

Ingeborg gives her mother a confused look before turning back around to face the woman at the door.

I'm a specialist at Haukeland University Hospital, she says smugly, so this area couldn't be any more perfect for us. We've got a little girl, she's three, she's going to be a big sister soon actually, so we're going to need all the play space we can get.

Nina shakes her head inwardly as she observes her daughter with growing discomfort. She might as well be wearing a pith helmet, whip in hand.

The woman stands in the doorway, stiff and silent. The boy whimpers, his mother picks him up and balances him on one hip, he clings to her, burrowing his face in her neck.

You'll have a few months' notice, obviously, Ingeborg says impatiently. But before we terminate the contract, I'd love to have a look inside.

If it's not convenient then we can come back another time,

Nina interjects, with what she hopes is a warm, apologetic smile.

It's not really a good time, the woman in the doorway says.

Just a quick peek? Ingeborg says.

I'm sorry, she says, shaking her head.

How many bedrooms are there, can I ask? Ingeborg says.

The woman thinks about whether she should answer the question or not.

Three, she says eventually, and Ingeborg looks starry-eyed.

Ingeborg, Nina says, then turns to the woman. I'm sorry that we've disturbed you like this, she says. We'll get in touch and arrange another time.

Does it have a fireplace? Ingeborg asks as Nina tugs at her coat sleeve to lead her away.

Please, the woman says, comforting her son.

I can assure you, Ingeborg continues imperviously, we really don't mind if the place is a little untidy.

It is as if the woman surrenders. She hesitates for a moment, then reluctantly steps to one side. Ingeborg makes her way in, unabashed, and follows the woman inside and upstairs without removing her boots.

Nina sighs silently and walks in after them, up the narrow staircase; she recognises the psychedelic, red cyclamen wallpaper. She vaguely remembers having visited once, many years ago, probably when Ingeborg was a baby. Aunt Lena had visited them numerous times, but very rarely returned the invitation.

As they enter the living room she thinks hard about where she might have seen the woman before. The boy is sitting on the floor beside a pirate ship.

It's like being in a museum, Ingeborg says. How long have you lived here?

Just over three years, the woman replies.

And you've never felt the need to change anything? Ingeborg asks, gesturing towards the room. Impressive.

I'm not all that interested in interior design, the woman replies curtly.

Is it alright if I have a little look around? Ingeborg asks, and the woman nods.

Nina stands in the middle of the room, uncertain, while the woman looks down.

I didn't properly introduce myself downstairs. Nina Wisløff, she says, offering the woman an outstretched hand.

Mari.

Things are silent for a moment as Ingeborg rushes back and forth, flitting from one room to the next with her coat flapping behind her.

Have we met? Nina asks after a short while.

I don't think so.

She might be a little younger than Ingeborg, but older than most of her students.

No?

The furniture in the living room is just as she remembers it. Old-fashioned, Norwegian armchairs, a teak table, a narrow, threadbare old sofa. The bookshelves belonged to Aunt Lena, but the old encyclopaedias and book-club novels from the 1970s are gone. Nina lets her eyes wander over the spines of the books that now fill the shelves, she sees works of poetry, philosophy, a surprising number of German titles, plus contemporary fiction. Parenting books. A large collection of LPs. A record player has been positioned on a table of its own over by the window.

The young woman's gaze follows Ingeborg as humming drifts across the room from the corner where the toys are kept.

How old is he? Nina asks.

He just turned three.

A lovely age, Nina says. I have a three-and-a-half-year-old granddaughter myself.

The woman says nothing. Nina stands there smiling, glancing in the direction of the kitchen. It's an original, untouched since the 1950s. Beside the kitchen table is a Tripp Trapp highchair and an ordinary kitchen chair. On the table is a pile of books, a stack of paper, a laptop, and three small, black notebooks. She's studying something, Nina thinks.

Ingeborg climbs down from the small attic space.

Do you remember what it says in your contract? she asks. How many months' notice you're entitled to?

No, I—

How quickly could you move out, do you think?

The woman looks at her quizzically.

We've got a bit of a situation on our hands, you see. Maybe we could make a small financial contribution if you managed to pack up in, say—

Ingeborg, Nina interrupts sharply.

But, the woman says, we don't have anywhere ... my little boy, Ask, he goes to nursery just along the road, we...

This is a decision for your father and I, not for you, Nina tells her daughter in a tentatively authoritative tone.

But Mum, Ingeborg groans, before turning back to the woman. Five thousand kroner?

I'm sorry we've disturbed you, Nina says. There's no need for you to see us out.

Ten thousand? Ingeborg says, as her mother nudges her downstairs.

The door slams behind them, and Nina tugs at Ingeborg until they are back out on the pavement.

Goodness, she was odd, Ingeborg says, prising herself free from her mother's grasp.

*She* was odd? Nina says. You were like a member of the Gestapo in there, ready to deport her and move in!

It's just the hormones, Ingeborg says. Nesting. You've forgotten what it's like.

Nina says nothing, seething with shame at her daughter's behaviour and frantically trying to put her finger on where she has seen the woman before. If she happens to work at the university, it'll be a catastrophe.

I'll come back with you to talk to Dad, Ingeborg says. *He* understands the need for haste.

*I'll* be the one to talk to your father, Nina says sharply.

But he doesn't listen to you, her daughter replies.

Mads is sitting at the piano looking serene as they walk upstairs.

And when exactly did you transform into a pair of torpedoes, hmm? he asks the two of them. Milja is about to give her grandad a hug but stops in her tracks when she hears his tone and hovers in the middle of the room, uncertain.

Nina makes her way into the kitchen with the food shopping without glancing over her shoulder at him, while Ingeborg, who is less sensitive to the nuances in his mood, heads in his direction and asks him the *exact* square footage of the house on Birkeveien.

Sit down, he says, nodding at the table.

Ingeborg pulls an iPad out of her handbag, which she passes to Milja before obediently taking a seat.

Nina emerges from the kitchen and sits down without a word.

Mads gets up from the piano stool and sits opposite them.

Firstly, he says dangerously quietly, if I don't pick up the phone on the first attempt, try again. Hm? Rather than charging ahead at full speed.

Ingeborg opens her mouth to object, but Nina kicks her under the table.

Secondly, he says, looking directly at his wife: What on earth were you thinking, taking this mercenary of a daughter of ours to Aunt Lena's house?

If you'd just let me explain... Nina says, but he lifts a palm and she seals her lips.

She said you were persistent and aggressive, Mads says to Ingeborg.

Who? Ingeborg asks.

Who? Mads repeats, chuckling under his breath. The poor woman you've been harassing! The one who's been living in Aunt Lena's house for three years without a single late rent payment.

Ingeborg, Nina says quietly, nodding at her. Tell him…

Mads looks at Ingeborg inquisitorially.

We've got silverfish, Ingeborg says gravely.

Nina shakes her head, resigned.

My God, Mads says, gawping and leaning back in his chair, rolling his eyes, who *hasn't*!

Not that, Nina says, the other thing.

He looks impatiently at his daughter and back again at his wife.

What, that I'm pregnant? Ingeborg asks.

Mads opens his mouth, stops, his eyes flicking back and forth between his wife and his daughter.

Is it true?

Yes, Nina says, staring insistently at Ingeborg, waiting for her to validate the fact.

Mads leans over the table.

Is that *true*? he says, smiling, bashful, looking down. He leaps up, walks around the table, wraps his arms around her and shakes her, she starts laughing. Milja looks up from the iPad screen, curious.

How many weeks? How is it all going? he asks, letting go of her. He takes hold of her shoulders and looks her in the eye, then strokes her hair.

I should have known, he says. Who glows like this in November, of all months?

Nina exhales with relief as Ingeborg regales her father with tales of her fatigue.

Birkeveien would be perfect for you all, Mads says. There are three bedrooms, you know, and plenty of space.

It's just a shame there's someone already living there, Nina says, interrupting.

He turns to face her.

Not anymore.

She looks at him quizzically.

Thanks to you, he says strictly, and Ingeborg looks at them hesitantly.

She asked to be released from her contract, he says. Clearly she'd rather be on the streets than risk running into you two again.

What? Ingeborg whispers, wide-eyed. She looks at her mother triumphantly, as if everything that had happened on Birkeveien had gone to plan.

When I decided to keep the house rather than selling it, it was with you in mind, Mads says. You and your family.

He breaks out in a smile.

Is it all sorted, really? Ingeborg asks, looking to her father and then to her mother. Her eyes are no longer gleaming with shame at being scolded by her parents, but twinkling with longing.

We'll let you know when it's ready for moving into, he says. In the meantime, you can put your place on Skuteviken up for sale. Make sure the silverfish smile for the camera.

He gets up.

Dad, please tell me you're not joking, Ingeborg squeals after her father, who makes his way out of the kitchen.

He returns with a chilled bottle of champagne and two glasses.

Nobody's driving today, are they? he asks.

But I can't drink, Ingeborg objects.

All the more for us, he says, cracking open the bottle with a pop.

# Tuesday 20th November

She studies every face in the auditorium, anxious that the woman from Birkeveien might turn out to be one of her own students, examining every inch of the room for dark, wavy hair.

With relief, she realises that she's not there.

Greek tragedy, she begins, portrays high-ranking characters who experience a transition from good fortune to poor fortune, ultimately leading to their own demise.

Her students sit before her, their gazes fixed on their laptop screens. God knows what they're actually up to, lounging about with their coffee cups and chunky scarves and round-brimmed spectacles.

This transition – *peripeteia* – represents the climax of the action, she asserts.

The odd pair of eyes is locked on to her, but the vast majority of the auditorium's stares are vacant, their eyeballs shining in the reflection of the bright-blue screens in front of them.

Tension is created by the tightening of the dramatic knot – *desis* – moving towards the sudden turning point. Following *peripeteia*, there is a fall, the knot begins to unravel – *lusis* – and things move in the direction of the final conclusive event. The catastrophe.

She clearly recalls her former students, lined up before her and shining like beacons during her lectures on Greek tragedy. There was a certain respect back then, an interest in the subject, she starts to think, then catches herself. Romanticising former students, the first sure sign that retirement is on the horizon.

Aristotle believes that *King Oedipus* is a prime example of its kind, she says, because *peripeteia* and *anagnorisis* occur simultaneously.

She pauses for effect.

And what is *anagnorisis?* she asks when nobody present bothers to do so. That is the critical point at which the hero, most often, acknowledges his true identity and exposes the true nature of the situation. It is a change that bestows the hero with knowledge and that can reveal either close kinship or hatred between characters, for instance.

A prime example of this occurs during the scene in which Oedipus acknowledges that he killed his own father, she says, allowing her gaze to wander over her students, seeing no reaction other than the odd raised eyebrow. Murder, catastrophe, is nobody going to bite?

Which results in Oedipus gouging out his own eyes, she says, clearly enunciating each syllable.

And what exactly incites all of this, the hero's tragic demise, the catastrophe in its entirety? she asks. *Hamartia.* 'To err', in Greek. A misstep. A miscalculation of the situation due to the hero's limited powers of judgement; people are imperfect, after all.

She looks out at the auditorium once again.

We mustn't confuse *hamartia* with *hubris*, arrogance. Disaster doesn't strike as a result of any moral failings or guilt on the part of the hero, nor due to any particular character flaw, but is simply the result of a fateful error.

Some of the students take notes, or at least she assumes that to be the case, but she imagines that the majority are ordering clothing online.

To err is human, she says, attempting to address her young students directly with a degree of reconciliation in her tone.

People fumble in the dark. We often have no notion of the full scope of our actions.

She draws breath.

And in that sense, people's position in the world is a fundamentally tragic one.

A hand, finally.

Yes? she says, grateful, bowing slightly at the young student.

Did that really happen?

Pardon me?

Gouging out his eyes like that?

Well, Nina says. This is a *tragedy*. It's poetry.

So, he *didn't*, then? the student replies, sounding disappointed.

He does so within the framework of the drama, but as I'm sure you are aware, it's not a *docu*drama.

The student looks at her with bewilderment.

Another hand, a different student this time.

Yes? Nina says enthusiastically.

Why does he do it?

Perhaps because he ought to have seen the connection earlier? she says. He hasn't been able to do so, or perhaps hasn't wished to understand his true identity. Oedipus sees nothing before he absolutely *has* to. But once his eyes are opened to the fact that he's married his mother and killed his own father, he seeks darkness.

Married his mother? someone in the front row blurts out. *What?*

We'll be looking at Sophocles' most infamous tragedy in more detail during our next lecture, she says dryly, closing the lid of her laptop.

Please welcome Professor Nina Wisløff, the moderator says, and she gets up from where she's sitting in the front row and joins the others on stage to the sound of applause.

She hasn't managed to prepare anything; hunger gnaws at her.

She's still brimming with indignation after the lecture, and when she takes a seat and looks out at the room, she's relieved not to see a single one of her students.

It's rare that she participates in panels like this, but she's stepped in at the last minute for a colleague she holds in high esteem. She lives according to her own pleasure principle, doing as much of what she likes as possible and as little of the opposite as she can get away with; as a result, she tends to politely decline invitations like this, whether they come from the university, the library, or, as is now the case, the House of Literature.

The field of literary studies belongs in dim, dusty offices with the blinds drawn, or in long-forgotten scholarly journals; it is ill-suited to being paraded on stage under the watchful gaze of every man and his wife. The cracks begin to show when you look too closely, Nina thinks from time to time, with significant unease.

Her fellow panellist, a professor of French literature, stands up and takes the mic before the moderator has a chance to introduce properly the three participants on stage.

'What is the purpose of literature?' he posits with gusto, reciting the evening's theme before pausing dramatically and letting his eyes wander over the faces in the audience.

In the words of Proust, he says, taking a deep breath: 'Real life, life finally uncovered and clarified, the only life in consequence lived to the full, is *literature*.' He closes his eyes for a few seconds to give the audience a moment to digest this mysterious paradox before sitting back down wearing an expression of self-satisfaction.

The moderator moves to respond, but the third panellist, a young, vivacious poet, takes the mic.

In my view, he begins, the ultimate indication that something ill thought through is bound to follow, in my view, he repeats, literature liberates us from tyranny! He announces it with a confident, serious expression, and a snigger slips out of Nina before she realises that he's being sincere.

Poetry is like a vaccine against oppression, the poet asserts, and Nina stares at the moderator in disbelief as he accepts this point of view without any further comment.

The poet concludes his declaration of literature's inherent anti-totalitarian powers of resistance as Nina squirms in her chair in intellectual discomfort.

Wisløff? the moderator finally says with a nod in her direction.

She straightens up slightly in her chair.

Now's the time to distance myself from this lot, she thinks to herself, then clears her throat.

My perspective is that of one who has spent a lifetime teaching literature, she begins. What is the purpose of literature? It's relatively obvious, I would say: literature exists to illuminate, to allow us to see ourselves, to entertain us. Case closed. For me, the more pressing question is this: what is the purpose of literary *scholars*?

She feels a shudder course through her as her words reverberate around her; too late now.

What use have we really for these more or less talented young people who spend so many years of their lives poring over literature? What exactly do they give back to society?

Out of the corner of her eye she sees the French professor raise an eyebrow.

A certain lively apprehension ripples through the audience. All eyes are on her. She knows that half are wondering if they're bearing witness to the early signs of dementia. The other half are current or recently graduated students from the university who assume this introductory statement is simply an interesting rhetorical move designed to rouse interest.

A handful of my students are hard-working young people, she begins, capable of detecting meaning in the most hopeless of ancient poetry. They produce extremely well-written, detailed essays on a random assortment of clumsy, poorly written novels. They ruminate, write at length, cite entirely incomprehensible theories, waffling on and on, Nina says, before pausing and wondering where her argument will lead her.

But for *what*? she asks, allowing a few more seconds to pass.

Half end up in a library, a publishing house or the media, spending the rest of their days nurturing their own particular interests. The rest never emerge from the world of academia, she says, her gaze fixed on the audience.

Imagine if they were to focus their intellect on something truly important! she says eventually, her voice shaking slightly. At the sound of the word 'important', the audience lets out a gasp.

The French professor indicates that he wishes to speak, but is held at bay by the moderator.

Take Magnus Carlsen, she asserts. We have this national chess-playing prodigy, this tremendous mind, yet we let it all go to waste on a *game*?

What concrete solutions do you propose? the moderator asks, and Nina realises that she has little left to lose; she's already taken an extreme standpoint. She perches on the edge of her seat and turns to face the audience.

What skills do literary scholars possess? she asks.

Reading and writing, someone in the audience chips in.

I think that was a rhetorical question, the moderator replies.

No, Nina says, it wasn't. And it's true enough, we do tend to be good at reading and writing, as a rule. What else?

No more suggestions from the audience, for fear that the question might be rhetorical after all.

Interpreting texts? she suggests. Finding meaning and making connections? She sees a few nods.

Reading literature in a number of different ways is a form of enquiry, she says, lowering her voice as she does when she wants her students to listen carefully.

There are mysteries and answers more or less concealed in every single text, doors waiting to be opened.

Her two fellow panellists have checked out of the debate by now and both study her with slightly pursed lips.

In reality... Nina says, looking out at the audience as she seeks a way to conclude her argument, ...in reality, literary scholars could make fantastic investigators.

The moderator looks at her inquisitively, and even she is un-certain whether she said the words out loud or merely thought them.

But surely that's exactly what your colleagues at the Norwegian Centre for Human Rights are engaged in, the moderator suggests. They study legal statements and rulings with exactly that, a literary focus, in order to expose miscarriages of justice.

*Expose*, Nina repeats with a snort. The task of literary scholars ought to be to *prevent* miscarriages of justice occurring in the first place!

What do you mean by that? the moderator asks, perplexed.

Literary scholars should be working for the police! Nina barks, so loud that she surprises even herself.

The moderator's eyes widen.

Are you being serious? he asks.

Serious? Nina says. Absolutely. We cannot entrust something as critical as police work to the police force! A literary scholar is capable of evaluating certain questions to an equal or likely an even greater degree than any police investigator: does the alleged motive make sense, for instance, or might the investigation have lost its way? What does an interviewee's choice of words and phrases reveal about them, what does it have to say about their psyche, their background, their way of life? A literary scholar is better suited than anybody to decide whether the story the police are telling themselves is credible or not, and they can do so while an investigation is under way.

Interesting, the moderator mumbles, and sounds as if he means it, though not in a positive sense. He nervously leafs through his notes.

Let's get back to, uh... he stutters, turning to face the French professor. What can literature teach us about life?

My God, take the Orderud case, for example, Nina interrupts with irritation. A triple murder, four suspects, all sentenced to serve time while a few of them continue to protest their innocence. How is it possible that *two* separate trials ended up with the least plausible explanation imaginable?

She doesn't wait to allow a response.

Because anyone with anything to do with the case – the investigators, the lawyers, even the jury – they all lacked something vital.

She pauses as everyone present waits with bated breath.

*A capacity for empathy*, she says. To read fiction is to empathise. Wouldn't you agree? Those who don't read receive no training in empathising with others. And the result? They are unable to understand people.

She takes a breath.

And *that* is the purpose of literature, she concludes.

Thank you for that, the moderator mutters meekly, turning to face the French professor once again.

She sits back in her chair, her pulse racing, doing her best not to look at the audience.

# Wednesday 21ˢᵗ November

She is woken by Mads. He sits at the foot of the bed in his suit, ready to leave, her mobile in his hand.

Congratulations, he says with a smile imbued with both solace and schadenfreude, passing her the phone.

She sits up and grabs her spectacles from the bedside table. Second from the top on the *Bergens Tidende* newspaper website is the headline: 'Professor calls for literary scholars to join the police force.'

No! she wails, pulling the duvet up over her head.

He pulls it back and Nina buries her face in her hands.

I don't think it's such a bad idea, actually, he says, and she glowers at him. But then I've never really understood your job. He places her phone down in front of her on the duvet and kisses her cheek before getting up and leaving.

She opens the link and feels her heart rate increase as she reads a feature written by the editor of the culture section.

'The most surprising input of the evening came courtesy of Professor of Literature, Dr Nina Wisløff,' she reads. 'The relatively anonymous academic – arguably better known as the wife of Mads Glaser, the health-board representative who opted to have his own house demolished, than for her own professorial merits – made an impassioned attack on her own field of expertise, which she characterised as being of little importance, a claim that left the audience rubbing their eyes in disbelief. The self-flagellating professor's crusade is to encourage literary scholars to enter the police force. It's easy to picture these bookish investigators in lively discussion about Adorno and Deleuze at the station while their fellow officers are left scratching their heads,' he writes, engaging in such flowery rhetoric that it's painful to read. She feels her face flush hot.

Fortunately she doesn't have any teaching scheduled today. She feels as if she's glowing like a beacon. She doesn't do media appearances. Contributing to subject-specific papers and the odd literary journal, sure, but appearing on the home page of one of the city's largest news websites? And championing a point of view she can't even really get behind, no less? A publication ban, she thinks to herself, next time, if there ever is a next time, I'll demand a publication ban.

She has two tutorials with master's students scheduled before lunch and is careful not to let the word 'important' escape her lips, but instead she praises her students' original arguments. In reality, she can't help but emit a slight groan when one of her students tells her that he's planning on researching crime in contemporary Norwegian poetry.

A slightly narrow focus, don't you think? she replies suspiciously. Is he making fun of her?

Do you think so? the student replies, unsure.

I can't think of many, if any, examples of *poetry* focused on crime, Nina says.

He looks at Nina with an odd expression on his face. *Rhyme*, he says. I want to look at rhyme in contemporary Norwegian poetry.

Oh, I see! Go for it, she says, getting up.

She bumps into the head of subject by the photocopier and lowers her gaze in order that she might get on with her photocopying in peace, but to Nina's great surprise she stops and pats her shoulder.

Excellent write-up, she says, winking at Nina in a very familiar manner. Initially Nina feels relief and a swell of pride, but then it hits her that the head of subject, recruited from a liberal-conservative think tank, now views her as an ally in the fight for continued instrumentalism in the humanities.

She spends the rest of the day shut away in her office to avoid the scornful or puzzled expressions of her colleagues. She replies to all of her emails to ensure that nobody can claim she isn't doing her job, and then she sits for an hour looking at houses listed online. With mixed feelings, she enters the search page and selects the various parts of town, types of property, square footage and price range. She wants what she's always had. When she hits the search button, nothing appears. There isn't a single house in the whole of Bergen that meets her criteria.

After adjusting her search to more accurately meet the realities of the property market, she wrinkles her nose: entire tenement buildings and grey, charmless, functional new-build houses miles from the city centre. She quickly scrolls down, shaking her head.

At around two o'clock, Ingeborg asks her if she might be able to collect Milja from nursery. Eagerly she grabs her coat and makes a dash for the door.

At the far end of Festplassen, she and Milja bump into Kaia and Jo, who are walking by the Lille Lungegårdsvann lake with their arms around one another. Kaia, almost skipping along and giggling in her floor-length wool coat, and Jo, looking deliberately unkempt in his distinctive spectacles and long coat.

What do we have here? A honeymooning pair of New York intellectuals straight out of an old Woody Allen film? Nina says.

Kaia crouches down and exchanges a few words with Milja while Jo leans in to kiss Nina on the cheek.

Good evening, fair sister-in-law, he says theatrically, as three days' worth of stubble prickles her cheek. Congratulations on the interesting piece in today's paper.

Kaia stands up and quickly embraces Nina. Nina catches the scent of perfume, warm skin, sparkling wine. The highlighted tips of her hair are dishevelled, revealing her dark roots.

If us psychologists are able to work with the police, literary academics should really be extended the same privilege, she says.

Surely the question is how the police will respond to your call to action? Jo says.

You're not off to Grieg Hall this evening? Nina asks, changing the subject.

Not as far as I know, Jo says, looking at Kaia.

No, that'd send us to sleep, Kaia says. You're not wondering why we're sauntering around, clearly inebriated?

That was going to be my next question, Nina says.

Let me introduce the new director of oncology, Kaia whispers into her ear.

Oh! Nina says, throwing her hands out in Jo's direction.

Nothing's official just yet, he says, gesturing for them to calm down. But we had to have a mini-celebration in advance.

A long lunch, Kaia says with a wink.

Wait a minute, Nina says to Milja, who's started tugging at her arm. That's worthy of celebration, she says. What are you up to this weekend?

We were talking about heading to the cabin up in Ustaoset, Jo says. They've had their first snow.

We're up for a change of plan though, Kaia says.

Mads and I are heading over to Oldervik, she says. Fancy joining us?

Sure, what do you think? Kaia asks, looking at Jo.

I've got a conference tomorrow and Friday, Jo says. Mads too, I think?

Whereabouts? Kaia asks.

Solstrand.

Well, it's on the way, so that works, Nina says.

The boys can take one car and the girls can take another, Kaia says, and Nina waves goodbye as Milja drags her away.

In an attempt to curry favour with Milja, she serves hot dogs for dinner, but her granddaughter gives them the merest prod before proceeding to spoon ketchup into her mouth.

Afterwards, Nina fetches pencils and paper, but Milja shows no interest: after scribbling briefly on the sheet of paper, she starts drawing on the table with a crafty smile.

Nina fetches a selection of old boardgames she's been looking forward to sharing with her granddaughter; Milja, for her part, insists that she wants to play on the iPad.

But Grandma doesn't have an iPad, you know that, Nina says, and her granddaughter gazes up at her with a combination of amazement and scorn. Nina is on the verge of trying to download some game or other onto her phone to satisfy her demands, but instead she attempts a cunning diversion tactic.

Time for some cocoa, I think!

Ice cream! Milja says, her hands by her sides.

It's not a grandparent's job to bring up children, Nina thinks afterwards, as they sit in front of the television, each with their own long-forgotten ice cream, discovered after a rummage around at the back of the freezer.

Ingeborg calls at that moment and asks if Milja can stay the night. She and Eirik are still in full swing, styling the apartment for photographs.

What's the secret to getting her to do as you ask? Nina asks.

Isn't Dad there with you?

He's going to be back late, Nina says.

Just give her the iPad.

I don't have one!

Ingeborg ends the call with a sigh.

In bed, Milja screams for Mummy and Daddy while Nina

frantically scans the bookshelves in the hallway for a children's book or collection of fairy tales. Eventually she stumbles upon an old copy of *Aesop's Fables*, which she plucks from the shelf and clutches tightly as she runs back into the room.

Milja objects obstreperously as Nina suggests one fable after another, *The Lion and the Mouse*, *The Fox and the Stork*. Eventually she reaches *The Hares and the Frogs*.

'The Hares were having such a terrible time that they decided to take their own lives,' Nina reads, and Milja falls silent.

Nina glances down at her and she looks back up at her grandmother. Nina is so relieved to have a moment's respite from her theatrical wailing that she reads on without hesitation, uncertain whether Milja understands what taking one's life actually means. She's never actually read this fable, so she's keen to find out how it will end after such an interesting start.

'The hares were tired of finding themselves under constant attack from other predators,' she reads, 'never able to enjoy a moment's peace without being plagued by fear. Was life truly worth living? The hares got together and eventually decided on a dramatic course of action: collective suicide.'

Milja rests her head on the pillow and listens intently, her eyes wide.

'The hares hopped down to a small lake nearby, where a group of frogs were crouching by the water's edge in the moonlight. Terrified by the gallop of the hare's paws as they approached, the frogs hopped into the water in a panic. The splashing of the frogs in the water caused the nervous hares to stop short on their way towards their planned death by drowning. One wise hare stepped forwards and said: Stop, my fine fellow hares. No matter how weak and afraid we may feel, there are creatures even weaker and more afraid than we are. Why should we end our lives? Let's make the best of this situation.'

And that was that, Nina says.

Another story! Milja says.

Another story? Very well, let me see, Nina says, glad to finally have some sort of upper hand over her granddaughter. Quickly she riffles through the book to find something that might capture her interest while also helping to put her to sleep. 'The Sick Lion', she says, and Milja nods gravely.

'King of the beasts, His Majesty the Lion, had fallen ill,' she reads. 'He lay in his cave, groaning and sighing. The other animals weren't sure what to do, now that they'd lost their leader. Eventually they decided to visit him, for if they failed to do so, he was sure to become enraged, and he was too ill to do them any harm.'

Milja lay there, rapt.

'One by one, or in small groups, they made their way to the royal cave. Some brought small gifts; others came only to speak with him. All creatures great and small visited the sick king,' she reads.

'Only one animal was missing: the Fox.

'As soon as the Lion realised that the Fox wasn't intending to visit him, he sent the Jackal to ask how he could be so inconsiderate.

'His Majesty is extremely unhappy with you! the Jackal said. There he lies, gravely ill, and you haven't even poked your nose in to see how he's feeling.

'Mr Jackal, the Fox replied solemnly. It's not that I don't wish to see our king. Quite the contrary! I value him as highly as everyone else. Several times now I've been on my way to see him, always with a little chicken bone as a gift—

'Yes, but then what happened? the Jackal asked impatiently.

'Well, then I spotted something that frightened me, something that stopped me in my tracks, in spite of how keen I was to pay the king a visit.'

She stops, looks down.

Milja is lying with her nose buried in the pillow, breathing deeply.

Thank goodness for that, Nina thinks. She places the book

down and perches on the edge of the bed for a long while to make sure that her granddaughter is really sleeping.

Eventually she turns out the light above the bed, stands up and tiptoes out of the room, letting the door close behind her, gently, gently.

By the time she arrives back downstairs, Mads is home. He's turned on the oven and is standing at the kitchen worktop making supper.

He gives her an inquisitive thumbs up and she nods with thinly concealed pride.

Fast asleep, she whispers.

Bravo, he says, pulling out a plate for her.

# Saturday 24th November

The two men are standing in front of the house in their work gear, Mads up a ladder, inspecting the eaves of the house, while Jo holds on to it at ground level, keeping it steady for his older brother.

Have a look at that, Kaia says. Men of the wilderness.

Jo waves at them in his flannel shirt, his brown hair dishevelled.

They'll have been sitting inside on their phones until about ten minutes ago, max, Nina says, turning off the engine. Let's not tell them we're on the ferry over next time.

They climb out of the car. Nina inhales the cold, clear air, deeply and with her eyes closed. Oldervik, the old farm and cabin on the isle of Tornøy, had been passed on to Mads by his mother, and they liked to spend as many weekends there as possible.

Well, well, well, if it isn't you two! Mads says, coming down the ladder. I'd welcome you with a hug, but, well... He holds up his gloved hands, which are covered in brown, soggy leaves from the gutter.

He cranes his neck in Nina's direction and kisses her cheek before she turns away and heads inside.

A warm blaze flickers in the old wood burner. Nina arranges pastries on a plate and sets the table.

They sit on the sofa in silence, sipping coffee and gazing out at the fjord. A still, cloudless sky shines a pale golden colour.

You wouldn't consider just moving out here? Kaia says, placing her mug down.

What would we do with ourselves? Nina says.

Oh God, Kaia says. Of course, I forget, you're joining the *police force*. And what about Mads, what's he going to be – hospital director? Spokesperson?

Or retiree, maybe? Jo says.

How was the conference? Nina asks.

Mads gave a boring talk on the future of national healthcare, Jo says. Key word: robots.

No one is irreplaceable, Mads says with a shrug.

Surely the simplest approach would be to replace the entire city council with a fleet of robots? Nina suggests.

But I did hear a good story from a former colleague yesterday, Mads says. One of the senior consultants we work with had spent a few days on the ward after having a benign tumour removed, nothing dramatic. There he lay, in his own department, surrounded by his colleagues. But when one of the nurses arrived to administer painkillers, he realised she'd brought him the wrong medication.

So what happened? Kaia asks.

He took them anyway, every last one. It wasn't long before he began to feel unwell, so he called someone over and explained the situation. 'But why on earth didn't you say anything?!' they asked him. 'I didn't want to be a difficult patient!' he replied.

Bloody hell, Nina says. I hope he was fired?

Very normal logic for any patient, Kaia said, unmoved. As a patient, you're put in your place from the very beginning. Firstly, you're bloody lucky just to be allocated an appointment – getting through on the phone is enough of a challenge. It's relentless from there on in: the patient has to be on time while the doctor turns up whenever it suits him...

I think you'll find it's our patients that delay us, Jo interjects.

Sure, but even so, she says, forging ahead, the doctor is healthy, the patient is ill. The doctor is strong, the patient is weak. The doctor speaks, the patient listens. The patient is interrupted, while it is the doctor who does the interrupting...

There was a study showing that three out of four patients are interrupted after just a few seconds, before they even have a chance to say what's wrong, Mads says.

*Eighteen* seconds, Jo says. Let's not exaggerate.

The doctor speaks in terms that the patient only ever understands to a certain extent. The patient, for their part, is required to lay bare the most intimate of details, Kaia continues. Then out of the blue they're required to undress. At any given moment they might suffer pain at the hands of the doctor, and so on and so forth. A patient is required to accept without question things that are entirely unheard of in wider society. They suffer a complete and utter lack of control.

And you submit yourself, Nina says. Afraid that you might be disliked by the doctor and that their dislike might affect your treatment.

Precisely, just like what happened with your colleague, Kaia says, nodding in Mads' direction. You're afraid of being viewed as a 'difficult' patient, so you ask as few questions as possible, avoid raising any objections and do your best not to cause any bother.

Though we do give you the gift of life in return, Jo retorts. Anyway, a little submission never hurt anyone.

Hmm, Kaia says. I'm just saying. As power structures go, you'll struggle to find another relationship as imbalanced as that which exists between doctor and patient.

So, is it official yet? Nina asks, turning to face Jo.

Is what official? Jo asks.

That you're the new director?

They're announcing it on Monday, he replies.

We'll have to toast the news properly later on this evening, Mads says.

Why wait? Nina asks, getting up. She makes her way into the kitchen and fetches four small glasses and a bottle of grappa from the top cupboard.

By the time she returns, the others are wearing grave expressions.

What is it? she asks, stopping in her tracks with the glasses and bottle in her hands.

We were just discussing one of our senior consultants, Jo says. We've been aware of it for years, but it's just been allowed to carry on ... Everyone's at fault, really. Not least the doctor in question, obviously, but—

And now the problem's landed in your lap, Nina says.

Grown adults with the capacity to save lives, Kaia says, yet somehow incapable of ignoring the odd clumsy comment.

Well, surely such comments are only ever intended as compliments? Mads replies mockingly as Kaia shrugs.

Well, I'm looking forward to this Me Too movement reaching you psychologists, Nina says to Kaia. *That'll* be fun.

Ugh, can you imagine? Kaia whispers. All those couches covered in semen.

Nina chuckles, shaking her head.

Either way, crystal-clear cases of abuse are few and far between, Kaia says. Have you been following the stories about that Swedish intellectual? Turns out the accuser had dinner with him on numerous occasions after the alleged rapes took place.

Well, we all need to eat, Nina says.

Either way, Mads says, raising a glass. Let's raise our glasses in a toast to my little brother.

## Sunday 25th November

She lowers herself gently into the warm water. Her body feels pleasantly worn out. They've climbed the highest peak on Tornøy in the same brisk autumnal weather as they experienced the previous day, they were able to see for miles in every direction, she had a clearer view of the glacier than she can ever remember having before.

They'd enjoyed Mads' venison casserole before Jo and Kaia set off in the car for home, Jo keen to prepare for the following day, when his new promotion would be made official.

Mads enters carrying two large glasses of red wine.

Aren't you going to be driving? she asks.

Not until this evening, he says, passing her a glass. Room for one more in there?

I can hardly say no.

He unbuttons his shirt and unbuckles his belt.

I'll never get over what this bath cost, she says.

English porcelain, he says, stepping in. Good quality doesn't come cheap.

The delivery charge alone... she says.

This bathtub was my way of breathing new life into our marriage, he says. And worth every penny, wouldn't you agree?

So our marriage is suffering oxygen deprivation, is that what you're saying?

It recovered nicely after making this purchase, he says, lying back and closing his narrow eyes.

Hilarious.

In our next house— he begins, but she interrupts him.

Let me guess. In our next house we'll have a bathtub? She takes a long sip of her wine before setting her glass down on the edge of the bath and lying back. She stretches out her legs; the bath is both long and wide, sufficiently generous in size for two adults to fit comfortably.

It wasn't the length or width that was important, he maintained when he lectured her on the merits of the bathtub after its purchase, keen to justify the exorbitant delivery costs. It was the depth. Being able to submerge your entire body without any limbs left sticking out of the water, *that* was what really mattered.

The tub had really been intended for the house on Fløenbakken, but it had turned out to be so heavy that the tradesmen felt there was a risk it might crash straight through the floor. Mads had even been willing to turn one of the upstairs bedrooms into a bathroom to accommodate it before they'd come up with the idea of moving it out here.

She thinks about the house on Fløenbakken. How strange it is, what's going to happen to it. Everything is to be packed up and moved out, her entire life, all transported to some unknown location. Like transplanting a brain into a foreign body.

Mads is less sentimental, he's a pragmatic sort. Not quite as tied to memories and the past, more easily moulded by his surroundings. He's adaptable, he embraces change.

What are you thinking about? he asks her.

The fact that I'm a dinosaur, she replies, and he raises an eyebrow inquisitively.

I'm no good at facing up to change, she explains.

The proposed light-rail track?

She nods.

That's the meteorite that'll wipe you out, he says, half smiling.

I was looking forward to growing old in that house. I hoped I might die there.

He fixes her with a studious gaze, water up to his chest, only his shoulders and head above the surface.

I've underestimated the situation, he says slowly. I've failed to grasp how difficult this is for you.

We're not the same, she says curtly.

I'm sorry, he says.

She shakes her head.

Yes, he says. I'm sorry.

You did everything you could.

Still, I could have thought more about just how much worse this feels for you than it does for me. It's your childhood home, after all.

It's like losing a life partner, she says, without warning, without any explanation. As if somebody had taken you from me and said: don't worry, plenty more fish in the sea!

He chuckles quietly, holding his glass.

Just the thought of replacing the allotment with a patch of asphalt... she says.

I promise you that I'll rustle up a garden for you, he says. No matter what else happens.

Promise?

Promise, he says, gently clinking his glass against her own.

She makes up her mind to broaden her search when she gets back home. Price, size, property type – and area, she thinks to herself finally, bringing her glass to her lips.

## Monday 26<sup>th</sup> November

The first half of the day consisted of a hair-raising strategy seminar at the university, a humiliating three-hour-long groupwork session during which they were supposed to brainstorm suggestions for improving the quality of their research.

When lunchtime eventually comes around, she sneaks away to the university library to pick up a book she's reserved.

By the entrance to the canteen she bumps into a retired colleague she always liked and sits down with her. They immediately begin exchanging horror stories about past strategy seminars, and by the time she finally manages to tear herself away, the second part of the seminar is well under way.

She decides to skip the remainder, settles on soup of the day for lunch and finds a table tucked away from other diners where she can leaf through a newspaper in peace.

She skim-reads the editorial and comments on page three, browsing the news section disinterestedly.

When she reaches page eight, she goes cold.

She recognises her immediately. It's the tenant from Birkeveien. She has longer hair in the picture, and she's smiling. But it's her.

She's gone missing.

Her name is Mari Nilsen. She's thirty years old.

She reads the short piece three times without drawing breath, her reading interspersed with fleeting recollections of the way she and Ingeborg had recklessly barged in just a week ago.

And now she's missing.

Nina brings a hand to her throat; she feels as if everyone around her can see that her arteries are fit to burst beneath her paper-thin skin.

Mari Nilsen has been missing since last Thursday. Three days after their unexpected visit. She had been visiting her parents on the isle of Tornøy. She had gone for a walk, but never returned. The police have no leads.

She's from Tornøy, Nina thinks to herself, that must be why she seemed so familiar, perhaps they'd seen her when they'd been in Oldervik, maybe she worked at the supermarket in the summer holidays, or at weekends.

One theory is that she returned to Bergen, she reads, but there have been no sightings of her on buses or ferries.

The police have issued a public appeal for information.

But what about her son, Nina thinks to herself, where is he?

She picks up the phone and searches her name; women and girls of all ages appear, none of them her.

She glances up to check that nobody is watching her. She searches her name and 'Bergen', then 'Tornøy', and that narrows the search slightly, but nothing relevant appears.

She searches her name in the phone book online, adding the address on Birkeveien. No Mari Nilsen; she's not registered at the address.

A growing sense of unease grips her, or worse, perhaps: guilt.

She should really contact the police and tell them about ... tell them about what, exactly? About the two unpleasant intruders who had called at the woman's door three days before she was last seen?

She leaves the library, her vision seems blurred, she cuts across the square diagonally as she calls Mads. He doesn't pick up, and shortly afterwards she receives a text: *In a meeting, anything urgent?*

She enters the Faculty of Humanities building and goes up to her office, where she sits at her computer and continues her search. She turns up a long list of hits, but none of the Mari Nilsens she finds are the right one, not even on social media, not one Face-book profile is a match.

As she prepares to type her name into the university email system, she feels her pulse begin to race. The idea that she and Ingeborg might have shown their true colours in the company of a junior colleague or a former student makes her stomach churn. She is relieved when her search comes to nothing.

Mari Nilsen's entire existence feels almost like a dream, though Nina knows all too well that she met her very recently.

She is on her way into the bathroom when Mads arrives home. It's half past eleven. He lugs his heavy work bag up the stairs and across the room before collapsing on the sofa in his suit with a sigh.

Aren't you coming to bed? she asks.

I think I need to sit up for a while, he says.

Can I get you anything? A drink, maybe?

He shakes his head before changing his mind. Do we have any beer in? he asks.

She goes into the kitchen and opens a bottle, handing it to him.

What a hopeless day, he says, pushing his spectacles up onto his head. My God.

She sits down across from him.

I've been trying to call you all day.

I'm sorry, he says with a sigh. I saw that. It's been non-stop, I visited the women's refuge, attended a seminar on welfare technology and then held a presentation on patient safety and user satisfaction, and that was all before lunch.

Have you seen the paper today?

I think so, he says. Actually, have I? I'm not sure, he says.

Did you see the picture of Mari Nilsen?

He looks up at her quizzically.

Who?

Mari Nilsen, our tenant, there was a picture of her in today's paper.

Really?

She's... Nina begins, and her voice starts to shake. He looks up at her. She's missing, she says, and her voice cracks.

He furrows his brow and looks at her, puzzled.

Missing?

She nods.

As in...?

Gone. She's disappeared.

What in God's name...? he says, sitting bolt upright. What happened?

I don't know, she says.

But what did it say?

Hardly anything, she says. She was visiting her parents on Tornøy last Thursday. She was supposed to be out for a walk, and then...

Was she from Tornøy? he asks.

I thought there was something familiar about her, she says, nodding. Maybe she worked in the shop there.

Silence falls. Mads shakes his head. Nina observes him furtively, feels a sense of unease surge through her.

Where did you get her details to begin with?

He looks at her.

It was Jo who knew her. Well, a colleague of his, actually.

How long had she been renting from us?

Three or four years, Mads says, trying to work it out.

Was she a single mother?

That was my understanding, he says, taking a sip of his beer.

It can't have been anything to do with us, Nina says quietly.

What?

The fact she's gone missing all of a sudden. Ingeborg and I turning up at her door, I mean?

Nina, come on, Mads says, surely you're not worrying about that?

It was a textbook eviction.

Hardly.

You know what Ingeborg can be like. She was awful, to be honest with you. If there's some sort of mental illness at play, our visit might have tipped her over the edge...

He says nothing.

The police haven't been in touch with you?

The police?

It would be perfectly natural under the circumstances.

Perhaps, Mads says. But hardly very useful. I've barely spoken to her. The rent has appeared in my bank account every month like clockwork.

It looks like Ingeborg and Eirik will have to shack up with their silverfish for a little while longer, Nina says. A fitting punishment, you might say.

But why?

This Mari has to be found before she can move out! she says.

But she already *has* moved out, he says.

What? Nina replies, pale-faced.

I received a message on Wednesday saying the keys were on the kitchen table. I let myself in with the spare on Wednesday evening, and the place was empty.

But how could she have moved out in two days? After living there for three *years*?

Don't ask me, Mads says. Aunt Lena's furniture and things are still there, obviously.

Don't you think the police might be interested in looking at the house, to be on the safe side?

Well, yes, he says. That's probably a good idea. I'll call them first thing in the morning.

And maybe don't mention the way Ingeborg and I... she suggests, trailing off. There's no need to involve us any more than is necessary.

She should go to sleep, really, Mads is breathing heavily beside her, but she can't put her phone down. She refreshes her search over and over again, checks every news outlet, but there's nothing new about the disappearance.

She mulls over their confrontation again and again, combing her memory for details, anything that might shed some light on what's happened.

She wakes in the middle of the night, possibly due to Mads' snoring, but possibly after dreaming about machines preparing to tear down the house while she and Mads are sitting at the dinner table, a bulldozer suddenly crashing in through the kitchen cupboard.

Her eyes open instantly, and all of a sudden it hits her.

She grabs her phone and types it into the search bar.

It's her.

That's it.

Several images glow brightly on the screen.

Nina can hear the sound of her own heartbeat.

Mari Bull.

She begins scrolling through the endless list of results, numerous photos of various kinds, with and without her violin, some action shots of her with the orchestra, a number of portraits, a record cover showing Mari Bull alone in a field of rapeseed. The results are mostly from Norway and Germany, concert write-ups, the odd interview.

It's her.

And she's been living in Aunt Lena's dusty old house crammed full of furniture.

Nina turns to Mads. He's fast asleep. She can't wake him over this. She wakes him anyway. She elbows him in the side twice and he grunts and turns to face her, opening his eyes, looking for answers.

Mari Bull, she says.

Huh?

It's Mari Bull.

He looks at her, confused.

What are you talking about?

Mari Nilsen is Mari Bull.

He pulls himself up onto his elbows, open-mouthed as he looks at her.

Bloody hell, he says slowly.

I'm right, aren't I?

You are, he says as it dawns on him too. We've seen her perform.

At Grieg Hall, she says.

The Brahms violin concerto? he says. I thought there was something familiar about her...

Me too.

What happened to her? he asks.

That's exactly what we don't know! Nina says.

No, but I mean: where did she disappear to?

That's the whole point, she says, vexed.

Not like that, Mads said. I mean, she was such a gifted performer.

Yes, she says.

But then everything went quiet, he says.

Yes. And now she's disappeared all over again.

# Tuesday 27<sup>th</sup> November

She stands in a cloud of steam and smoke, browning meatballs and simmering spaghetti while Milja amuses herself at the kitchen table with her painting things. Ingeborg and Eirik are meeting with their agent to plan the sale of their house.

She taped a thick, textured sheet of card onto newspaper, dampening it carefully, and patiently showing Milja how to dip the paintbrush in water and then in the watercolour paints to create a beautiful, flowing play of colours on the sheet of paper.

It had taken less than ten seconds for her granddaughter to scrape the paintbrush so hard against the paper that it had fallen apart, after which she mixed all the colours together and took great glugs of the filthy water she'd been instructed to dip her brush in.

They didn't find anything of interest, Mads says, appearing at the door out of the blue.

Who? she says. What?

The police. They went through the whole house, he says, putting his bag down on the floor.

He places the keys on the kitchen worktop in front of her.

So it's ready for Ingeborg?

That's what they said, Mads says, hugging Milja.

So, what have you been painting? he asks her, sitting down. Your hands?

Milja sticks the paintbrush in the glass of water, then in the red paint, and finally into her mouth as she giggles defiantly.

Yuck, Mads says, ruffling her hair. Last one to set the table smells!

On hearing Mads' words, Milja flies from her chair like a bullet and makes for the sideboard, yanking out the drawers and pulling out three plates, which she obediently carries to the kitchen table as Mads promptly tidies away the painting things.

She just wrecks the joint whenever she's with me, Nina says, draining the spaghetti. How do you do it?

Life's unfair, he says, helping Milja to arrange the plates on the table. Certain people just have a way with children.

She rolls her eyes and places the food on the table.

They help themselves to meatballs, spaghetti and tomato sauce in silence. Milja gobbles her own portion greedily.

And how was your day? Mads asks.

She shakes her head.

A few tutorials first thing, she says, but after that...

He looks at her.

You've been googling Mari Bull all day, haven't you?

Yes, she admits.

I thought so. Anything new?

Nothing, she says. Just the same old stuff, I've been trying to find out why she went quiet.

And?

She shrugs and tries to remember what she read earlier in the day. In her mid-teens, Mari Bull had stepped back from her music studies in Oslo after being discovered by a prestigious music academy in Hamburg. After that, she move to Frankfurt, then debuted as a soloist at the Staatskapelle Dresden at the age of twenty-one.

She had met Norwegian conductor Niklas Bull in Germany, Nina read in an in-depth interview, and they married there six years ago, when Mari was twenty-four. In another interview printed in Tornøy's local paper, she read that the couple had left Europe two years earlier and moved into an older property in northern Tornøy. They intended to keep it as a base for their future careers and family life, Niklas Bull was quoted as saying.

But things had been quiet over the past three years.

Now her name was Mari Nilsen; she lived alone in Bergen with her young son, and had been reported missing by her family.

Ingeborg and I are probably the last people to have seen her, she says.

She thinks again about the fact that she, too, ought to talk to the police, but decides that she doesn't really have anything useful to share. All she would succeed in doing would be to incriminate herself: Why had she allowed her pit bull of a daughter to scare her away? That would be the question she'd have to face.

Missing for five days, Mads says slowly. That's quite a while.

She nods.

So, nothing, then? she asks.

What? he asks, looking up.

The police. They didn't find anything in the house?

No, he says, shaking his head. I was interviewed too, or whatever they call it, it was only very brief.

Really? Did you say anything they seemed to find interesting?

I don't think so, unfortunately.

Did *you* learn anything?

They can't say much. But I got the impression that they had very little to go on. Very few sightings, very few leads at all.

Strange.

But they were very interested in what kind of impression I had of her, how she had come across to me. Reading between the lines, there might have been some mental-health issues at play.

A vulnerable genius, Nina says.

Child prodigies do tend to struggle sooner or later, Mads says.

So Ingeborg and I are beyond suspicion? Nina says.

He laughs.

Relax, he says. I didn't say anything.

She takes a sip of her water to conceal her relief.

Fairy tale! Milja says suddenly.

Oh yes, Nina says. I've got a really spooky one to read to you tonight.

Anything on the house front? Mads asks.

Not a thing. Just tenements and soulless, functionalist new builds. I should have started the search ages ago. You knew where things were headed.

Have patience, Mads says. We still have time on our hands.

A *little*. It's either that, or we end up in a flat on Mannsverk.

I won't hear a bad word said about Mannsverk, Mads says. It'd make for a short commute for me, in any case.

So you *are* going back to work at the hospital, then? she asks with surprise.

I don't know, Mads says. We'll see how the land lies after the election.

But you'll almost certainly be elected for a new term?

Hard to say, he says, popping a meatball into his mouth.

Finished! Milja shouts, hopping down from her chair. Nina springs after her with a cloth in hand as Milja flies towards the sofa like an arrow, her face and hands covered in tomato sauce, her devilish laughter reverberating throughout the house.

# Saturday 1<sup>st</sup> December

Eirik and Milja stand on the steps and form the welcome committee as she approaches the house. Eirik is holding a glass of something sparkling and reaches out to hand it to her, while Milja clutches a carton of chocolate milk in one hand, which she eagerly slurps through a straw.

A Christmas wreath has been hung on the front door. Ingeborg certainly hasn't wasted any time getting settled.

Nina leans down to give Milja a hug but her granddaughter turns her back on her and sticks her nose in between her father's legs.

Fair enough, Nina says, taking the glass and giving Eirik a hug instead.

Congratulations on your new home, she says, clinking her glass gently against his.

Come on in, Eirik says, and she follows him and Milja inside and upstairs.

They find Ingeborg in the 1950s-style kitchen, feverishly red in the face. She's managed to dig out one of the old, heavy, crystal cake stands, onto which she carefully slides a marzipan cake.

Goodness me, Nina says. Not suffering any nausea then, I see?

Where's Dad? Ingeborg asks without looking up at her mother.

He had to work. What can I do?

Nina carries cups and plates into the living room, where Milja is sitting on the floor with her doll, having a tea party with one of Aunt Lena's old tea sets. Eirik takes the crockery from her and sets the old teak coffee table.

It's going to be lovely here, Nina says, looking around.

Eventually, Eirik says. We'll take it one step at a time.

Nina takes a seat on the old burgundy-coloured sofa. Stacked one on top of the other on the windowsill are two books about tidying up.

There are certain aspects to the interior design that jar with Ingeborg's taste, shall we say, Eirik murmurs, nodding in the direction of the hessian walls.

She takes a sip of her drink and thinks back to all the various draughty dumps that she and Mads had put up with until they were finally able to take on the house on Fløenbakken just after Ingeborg was born.

There, Ingeborg says, placing the cake on the table.

Each of them eats their own generous wedge of the enormous cake as Ingeborg and Eirik enthusiastically talk over one another about their plans for the house.

It's all going to the Salvation Army, Ingeborg says coolly, throwing an arm out across the room. Don't suppose you need a pink bathtub?

Ask your father, Nina says.

And then there'll be tradesmen coming back and forth for two months at least, Eirik says.

Surely you're not planning on living here while the work is going on? Nina asks, sceptically.

We'll stay where we are on Skuteviken until everything is finished here, obviously, Ingeborg says.

Where exactly *we'll* go when the demolition starts on our house is another matter altogether, Nina says.

Your problem is that you think you need a spacious family home, Ingeborg says. There are so many stylish, practical apartment complexes out there these days. You need to broaden your horizons.

Nina sighs loudly.

Oh, I meant to ask you, Ingeborg says, nodding at a cardboard box just outside the kitchen, would you mind passing that on to the woman who lived here before?

What?

It was in the cellar.

Nina gets up and makes her way over to the box.

Didn't the police look down there? she asks with surprise.

The police? Ingeborg says. What are you talking about?

Milja glances up inquisitively at the sound of the word 'police'.

You haven't heard? Nina asks, slowly.

Ingeborg looks at her, perplexed.

The woman who lived here... Nina says, looking at Ingeborg. She's gone missing.

Missing?

Eirik looks from Ingeborg to Nina, his brow furrowed.

Don't you read the paper? Nina asks, picking up the cardboard box and placing it on the dining table.

What's happened? Ingeborg asks.

Nobody knows. She's gone, the police are looking for her. She was last seen a few days after we were here.

Nina opens the box and peers inside: paperwork and a couple of ring binders.

Ingeborg's expression darkens.

That's odd, she murmurs under her breath. She stands up and makes her way towards Nina.

Yes, very odd, Nina says.

No, Ingeborg says, shaking her head. I mean...

What?

I came back a few days later, Ingeborg says quietly in order that Eirik won't overhear.

You did *what*? Nina asks.

I thought I'd offer to pay her removal costs. I stood there for ages ringing the bell.

Really? And? Nina says, feeling her pulse begin to race. What's her tactless daughter done now?

No answer, she says. It was pitch-black inside. All I could do in the end was walk away.

But? Nina says, sternly.

But I got chatting to a man, Ingeborg says, taking a seat at the dining table. While I was at the door.

A man? Nina says, pulling out a chair for herself.

He passed me a few times, walking back and forth. Eventually he approached me and asked me if I knew her.

So, what did you say?

He was trying to get in touch with her. They'd agreed to meet, apparently, but he'd heard nothing since.

What day was that?

Ingeborg thinks for a moment.

We were there on the Monday, weren't we? she asks.

That's right, Nina says.

So it must have been the Thursday, in that case, Ingeborg says.

My God, Ingeborg. That was the day she disappeared, her mother says. You don't know who he was?

No idea.

But what did he look like, how old was he, did he look dodgy?

Oh yes, Ingeborg nods, very dodgy. Like some sort of cartoon villain.

What?! Nina cries. We need to tell the police about this!

Mum, I'm *joking*, Ingeborg says with an expression of resignation. He was a totally normal-looking guy. Handsome. A little older than me. He seemed anxious.

Anxious how?

Anxious how? Ingeborg repeats. Anxious like anybody might seem anxious, hands in his pockets, shoulders up by his ears. He stayed behind after I left.

She stands at the dining table in the house on Fløenbakken and goes through everything from Mari Nilsen's box, the pile of ring binders, the loose paperwork and notepads that Mari Nilsen had hauled from one place to the next since the day she'd moved away from home, eventually arriving in the house on Birkeveien via Germany and Tornøy.

The largest ring binder is filled with certificates, bank statements and even more loose paperwork. Most of it dates back more than five years, but at the very bottom of the pile is something that's just a couple of years old, from November 2016.

Printed at the top are the words *Aponia Books*. Nina skim reads the text on the page, it's a contract, a freelance agreement with a publisher in town, signed by both parties. Editor, Mari Nilsen. Editor, Mari Nilsen? Could the box belong to another Mari Nilsen? she wonders, confused, shaking her head and setting the contract to one side.

She doesn't want to pry, but three identical notebooks under a folder of bank statements arouse her interest. They're the same as the ones she'd seen on the kitchen table, all three are small and bound in black.

Carefully she opens one of them, and her heart instantly begins to race as she realises that the lined, light-yellow pages are filled with dated entries.

The sloping handwriting is elegant, almost old-fashioned in appearance. Nina quickly scans the brief notes, but after leafing through all three notebooks, she is forced to conclude with disappointment that they must be nothing more than some sort of practice notes or something along those lines, all three filled with musical terms, *vivacissimo*, *allegro assai*, and so on and so forth.

She slips one of them into her bag, pretending to herself it's an absent-minded accident, then carefully returns the other two to their box.

The bank statements in the ring binder are unremarkable, she leafs through them quickly; there are letters to confirm Mari Nilsen has been accepted onto various courses of study here and there, all in German, as well as the odd employment contract for various orchestras, as far as she can make out. She thinks back to her field trip to Copenhagen, it was spring 2015. Yes, it must have been at some point that spring that Aunt Lena had died and Mari Nilsen had moved into the house. Mari Nilsen had been pregnant by then, and all alone, according to Mads. Where had Niklas Bull been at that point?

She clenches her jaw. He walked out on her when she was pregnant. You hear about that kind of thing from time to time, fathers who abscond in the middle of a pregnancy, whether out of panic or something more calculated, and there could be good reason for it, but it certainly didn't look good.

Or perhaps the opposite was true, perhaps it was Mari Nilsen who had left Niklas Bull, a man whose true nature ultimately came to light? Conductors, she thinks to herself, posers with oversized egos who smugly wield their batons, commanding an entire orchestra, their hair clinging to their sweaty foreheads.

Where in the world is Niklas Bull now?

She looks through the file one more time to see if she can find anything relating to child custody, contact with lawyers, social services or anything of that nature, but there's nothing to be found.

She wonders for a moment if the nature of the box's contents is such that she ought to hand it over to the police, but concludes that it probably isn't necessary. Anyway, Mads has already been interviewed on their behalf, that'll have to suffice.

She casts another glance at the contract from Aponia Books, then picks up her phone to look them up and immediately finds their website. Colourful book covers for titles on mindfulness, bacterial flora and specialist diets leap out at her.

She's familiar with the Greek word *aponia* – after all she's had a lifelong enthusiasm for Greek classics. If she's remembering correctly, it means 'absence of pain', physical as well as psychological, something along those lines, and was the most important aim for the Epicureans. Based on the description on the company's website, the pair behind the publishing house successfully achieved this aim long ago.

As she scrolls down the page, a black-and-white portrait photograph of the two smiling publishers appears. She immediately recognises one of them.

# Monday 3rd December

Aponia Books has a tiny office in the middle of Fosswinckels gate, with a large window beside the entrance, facing out onto the street. As Nina makes her way in, she sees two men in conversation at a Formica table, each sitting with his own paper cup from the coffee shop a few metres down the road and a plastic container of salad, both wearing black-rimmed glasses and black, tight-fitting jumpers.

The premises comprise an area of barely twenty square metres, with two writing desks and an enormous printer that fills the whole room with the scent of warm paper. She immediately recognises Tor, a former master's student, and he breaks into a smile as he catches sight of her.

My word, he says, pleasantly surprised, then quickly looks shame-faced as Nina's gaze sweeps over the books on display around them.

Yes, I've taken a break from *The Odyssey*, as you can probably tell, he says apologetically.

Ah, that's all right, Nina says, to be honest it's nice to see a former student who might actually be making a decent living for himself.

He smiles, relieved, and nods in the direction of his colleague, who gets up and introduces himself as Joakim.

What can we do for you? Tor asks after a few minutes of small talk.

She outlines the reason for her visit, and they raise their eyebrows as she explains that Mari Nilsen was her tenant.

And then I saw her picture in the newspaper just a week after meeting her, she concludes. It was a huge surprise, she adds quickly.

Yes, we're in shock ourselves, Tor replies.

And now I'm left here with a box of her things that I think her family ought to have.

But she's not *dead*, Joakim protests.

No, of course not, Nina replies sharply, that's not what I'm saying.

Mari's family? Tor says.

Yes, I was hoping you two might be able to give me a name. Something that might help me get in touch with a relative of hers.

They look at one another, inquisitive, both shaking their heads. No?

They're silent before Tor begins to chuckle. I'm a little embarrassed, he says, realising how little we actually know about her.

But she was very private, too, Joakim interjects.

Was? Nina says.

*Is*, he says. God.

Tor nods in agreement.

But she worked here? Nina asks, scanning the tiny premises.

Neither of us were very close to her, Tor says apologetically. Most of our contact was via email.

What did she do for you?

Just bog-standard proofreading, Tor says.

Seven or eight titles every six months, maybe, Joakim says.

How did you find her in the first place?

The usual way, Tor says. We put an ad out on social media and our website. We received applications from her and a few others, but when she revealed that she had a decent knowledge of German, she became the strongest candidate.

We publish quite a few German titles, Joakim adds.

So, she translated books, in addition to proofreading manuscripts?

No, but she provided good all-round quality control, he says.

Have the police come to speak to you?

Yes, Tor nods, and Nina feels slightly disappointed to discover that the police have also managed to track down the publisher.

But we were just as little help to them as we are to you now, Joakim says.

Income from her publishing work in addition to her child benefit, she thinks, plus child maintenance, possibly. It's not much. She reminds herself that she needs to ask Mads what Mari was actually paying in rent each month.

Oh well. I don't know what I'm looking for, really, Nina says. But it piqued my curiosity to discover she'd been working for a publishing house. She's a trained violinist, as I'm sure you're both aware.

Really? they both reply, looking at one another.

Nina takes a step towards the door.

She was due to have a go at translating something for us, actually, Joakim says.

*Is* due to, Tor says, correcting him, and Joakim flushes red.

It was her suggestion, he adds.

Really? What was – *is* – she working on?

It's curious, actually, Joakim says. It was her idea.

We have a series of classics, Tor says, suddenly a touch prouder of his publishing enterprise. We publish novellas of one hundred pages or fewer that fit within the rather wide-ranging genre of 'body and mind'. Reading material for the niche market.

He turns to Joakim: Wasn't it the Freud stuff?

I've got it here somewhere, Joakim says, shuffling and shifting piles of paper on his desk.

Tor makes his way over to the printer, where yet more stacks of paper lie.

Here we go, he says, brandishing a small pile. A selection of early articles by Freud. Fancy a peek? he asks, and she takes the papers he passes her. German.

Freud? she asks, surprised. And this was her idea?

That's right, Joakim says. She was planning on writing an introduction, too.

But she didn't have a background in psychology, did she? Nina asks.

They look at one another.

Didn't she? Tor asks, and Joakim shrugs. Nina thanks them and slips the wad of paper into her bag.

Call us if you hear anything, Tor says.

Ingeborg rings just as Nina is making her way up the steps at Nygårdshøyden.

What's happened? Nina asks, out of breath; as a rule, her daughter only ever calls in extraordinary circumstances.

He's in the paper, Ingeborg says. Today.

Who is?

The man I spoke to outside the house that evening, Ingeborg says, sounding frantic. On Birkeveien...

Really?

It's an interview, in the culture section.

In *Bergens Tidende*?

Yes, she says. I'm sitting in the canteen and just caught sight of his picture, it's him, one hundred per cent.

What's his name? Nina asks, picking up her pace.

Niklas Bull.

That's her ex-husband, Nina says quickly, and hears her daughter let out a little gasp.

That's it, it's *always* the ex-husband, Ingeborg says. Always the ex or the husband who's done it.

Nina doesn't bother playing dumb and asking 'done what?'. Instead she ends the call, jogs up the last few steps and hurries over the gravel just outside Johanneskyrkja.

Today's paper is sitting just by the coffee machine, untouched and unsullied; she grabs it and makes straight for her office, closing the door behind her.

It's him. Niklas Bull. He's been photographed outside Grieg Hall wearing a black pea coat, sunlight dappling his face. He has medium-length dark curls, just like his son, and is wearing a contemplative half-smile.

She quickly skims the interview, first in order to see if he makes any mention of Mari Nilsen – or Bull – but there's nothing to be seen, then to find out why he's been given a double-page spread in the first place: he's been announced as the new principal conductor of the Bergen Philharmonic Orchestra.

He's forty-one years old, she reads, and has been living in Oslo for the past few years, where he's conducted the Oslo Philharmonic. Prior to that, he spent a period of time travelling Europe and conducting one elite orchestra after another. Now he's landed his dream job, he asserts with a smile. Conducting the Bergen Philharmonic feels like coming home.

No mention is made of any other ties to the city. No missing ex-wife or three-year-old son.

She sits there and gazes vacantly into space, her head spinning. He walks out on his young wife when she's pregnant, travels all over, brazenly conducts orchestras here, there and everywhere, and all while his wife moves to Bergen alone? Then the child is born, a few years pass, and all of a sudden, he materialises once again, first in the city, then on her doorstep. The very same day that she is last seen.

Nina turns the page and finds herself looking at his face yet again, this time as part of an advertisement for his debut as principal conductor of the Bergen Philharmonic Orchestra in just two days' time.

She hops online and immediately checks to see if there are any tickets remaining. She secures two by the skin of her teeth.

## Tuesday 4<sup>th</sup> December

He is sitting beneath a patio heater in the beer garden behind the pub on Kong Oscars gate, wearing the same pea coat as in the picture. A box of *snus* is sitting on the table in front of him, along with half a cup of coffee. He looks up at her with a friendly smile as she stops beside his table.

There you are, he says, half standing up and taking her hand.

He pulls out a chair for her. They're all alone in the beer garden. The notion that this might actually have been a dangerous meeting to arrange flits across her mind.

Thanks for meeting me, he says.

My pleasure, Nina says, taking a seat. But I'm afraid that I don't really have much to tell you.

Something is better than nothing, he says with a despondent smile. She was your tenant for almost four years, you must have some sort of impression of things, at the very least.

We had very little contact, Nina mumbles.

What day was it that she moved out, did you say? he asks.

The day before her disappearance.

The Wednesday? he asks.

That's right.

That's what's so strange about it all, he says, looking at her. She and I were due to meet on the Thursday.

At her house?

That was ... the most convenient option. She has her son to think about, he goes to bed early. And my days are busy with orchestra business. I waited outside for ages, but nobody answered.

Sent messages, called, nothing. Later I heard that she was at her parents' house on Tornøy when we'd agreed to meet.

With her parents, that's right, Nina says, and he nods.

So you were in touch quite a bit, then, Nina says cautiously, looking at him.

We'd just resumed contact.

But you hadn't seen each other face to face for quite some time?

Not for many years, he says, shaking his head. But we'd started writing to one another now and then.

They sit there in silence.

When did you last see her? he asks eventually.

The Monday of that week, Nina says quickly, hoping he won't ask about the circumstances under which they met.

How did she look? he asks instead.

How did she look? she repeats. Well, I don't know how she normally looked.

Did she look well?

Fit and well, to my mind, she says. It certainly didn't occur to me that she wasn't in good health.

He nods, rubs his chin.

But what about the boy? she asks. Where is he now?

You mean Ask? He's with her parents. They're a nice pair, he's in good hands.

That's good, she says. As I mentioned on the phone, I've got a box of Mari's things that she left in the house when she moved out.

Yes.

Perhaps I ought to hand it over to her parents? she says, and he nods.

What are their names?

Sigrid and Toralf, he says, extracting a pouch of *snus* from under his top lip and tucking it away inside the section of the lid intended for used pouches.

Nilsen?

Nilsen, he confirms, stuffing a fresh pouch of *snus* under his top lip.

It has a familiar ring to it. She mutters their names under her breath to prevent herself from forgetting.

He sits there, fiddling with his tin of *snus* without meeting her eye.

It doesn't appear that they have anything else left to discuss.

She waits before getting up to leave. Takes a deep breath.

Do you have any idea what might have happened? she asks.

He looks up at her.

To Mari?

He shakes his head.

No idea at all? she asks.

None, he says. Really. As I say, we were supposed to meet that day. She never appeared. That's all I know.

She says nothing.

They interviewed me, he says. He stares into the distance with a look of self-pity on his face.

They came to my flat, took my computer, my phone...

He runs a hand through his dark curls.

They went through all of our messages, he says, can you even imagine? They went back years, back to the day we separated. Hardly a pretty picture.

He gives a resigned chuckle.

But you were on speaking terms again? Or, *are*, I mean, she says, catching herself.

Yes, he says.

Looking to patch things up?

I don't know, he says. I think so. That was part of the reason I took this job. The concert on Thursday, it'll be my nod to her.

Your nod to her? Nina repeats, but he says nothing.

There's a ticket at the door with her name on it, he says, staring into thin air with a sorrowful expression.

But now... he says, then falls silent.

# Wednesday 5<sup>th</sup> December

The box sits in the back seat, as if Nina were chauffeuring some sort of VIP around.

As she arrives on Tornøy and drives off the ferry she suddenly has cold feet.

She hasn't made any arrangements, but she has an address. For some reason or another, she can't face the idea of contacting them in advance, and instead decides to turn up without warning, as if by coincidence.

According to the map, Sigrid and Toralf live in the housing estate up by the college.

After driving twenty minutes along the fjord, she turns off the E39 and drives in the direction of Oldervik, parking her car in front of the house and carefully carrying the box out of the car.

She carries it through the park by the college, which will be in full bloom in just a few months' time. But now the enormous trunks loom huge and dark and dense. She crosses the road and nervously makes her way through the housing estate, glancing around in an effort to locate the couple's names on one of the post boxes as she passes.

Eventually she catches sight of their house number: it's one of those houses designed by architects in the 1980s, stained black cladding with large windows, angular, dynamic, yet oozing stylish simplicity.

Behind a dense and well-maintained hedge of winter foliage, the garden lies dormant. The beds are greyish-brown in colour and have been covered with thick layers of leaves, while bright purple and pink clusters of heather peep out of large, blue pots sitting on the small, old stone steps.

She begins to regret her decision before she even presses the bell, but here she stands nonetheless, and she hears it chime throughout the house.

Immediately she hears thudding on the floor upstairs. Ask. At the window she can make out an adult figure hurrying after the grandchild, perhaps to prevent him taking a tumble down the stairs.

The three-year-old reaches for the door handle, the heavy door swings slowly open. Nina suddenly feels anxious that he'll remember her from before. She hadn't thought about that. Perhaps he's capable of expressing what happened at their last meeting. She looks down with a smile as the little boy appears at the door.

Ask looks up at her with hope in his eyes before his face falls and he begins to cry.

Nina stands there with the box in her arms and stares down at the little boy with a stiff expression.

A tall, white-haired man appears behind the crying boy.

There, there, he says, picking him up.

Nina swallows.

Toralf Nilsen ruffles his grandson's dark hair and Ask buries his face in his grandfather's neck.

I'm Nina Wisløff, she says, and she feels herself begin to tremble as she offers him an outstretched hand, the box balanced on the opposite hip.

He nods, he recognises her, and the same is true for her, she remembers him from her younger days, back when they were loose acquaintances at college, and more recently from seeing him in the shop when she and Mads have been in Oldervik, all of which puts them on nodding terms of some sort. His black hair and beard have turned white, but he is otherwise as tall and slim as he was back in the seventies, though now slightly stooped.

He looks at Nina apologetically.

It's not your fault, he says with a weak smile, someone here misses his mummy and is hoping she'll ring the doorbell one of these days.

I don't mean to disturb you, she says, holding out the box in his direction. Your daughter ... she was our tenant.

Mari? he says in a surprised tone, immediately taking the box. Come in, come in, he says, stepping to one side as best he can as he pulls Ask in close.

Sigrid! he calls upstairs, before turning to face her.

Have you heard anything? he asks. Is there any news?

I'm sorry, she says, shaking her head.

She follows him and his grandson into the hallway. He places the box on a chest of drawers and nods in the direction of the staircase. Her heart skips a beat when she thinks about the notebook she tucked away, struck by the sudden fear that she might be discovered. Why did she do it?

Just head on up, he says. She's in the sitting room.

She looks up with surprise as Nina climbs the staircase. She removes her spectacles and places them on the coffee table in front of her, stands up.

It's you, is it? she says, her voice low as Nina desperately tries to recall how they know one another. She vaguely remembers knowing a Sigrid Nilsen many moons ago, like a faded photograph in an old album. Long, shiny hair, tanned skin. What else? Nina dredges her memory as it becomes ever clearer that the woman is having no trouble placing her.

We were at college together, Nina says, it seems the most plausible explanation.

Indeed we were, the woman says with a half-hearted smile, you've got a good memory, and Nina exhales, relieved.

Toralf comes upstairs with the box in his arms before placing it on the dining table. Ask follows his grandfather around like a shadow, hiding behind him and peeking at Nina between his legs.

Yes, you probably weren't aware, but your daughter was our tenant, says Nina.

On Birkeveien, do you mean?

Sigrid looks at her.

She left this behind, Nina says, nodding at the box, and Sigrid turns to the dining table, looking inquiringly at her husband. He shakes his head.

I don't know if there's anything there... Nina says apologetically.

I'm heading off now, Toralf says. Nice to see you, Nina.

He heads downstairs. Sigrid takes Ask by the hand and leads him over to his toys before making for the dining table, lifting the contents from the box and spreading them out across the table.

Nina looks around her. Bold artistic prints hang from the walls.

The old wooden floorboards are light in colour and recently polished.

Eventually Sigrid glances up at her.

Sorry, she says. I should have offered you a coffee.

No, no, of course not, Nina says, realising that Sigrid has been as unable as she was to find anything useful among the stacks of paperwork and files.

Have a seat, Sigrid says, gesturing towards the sofa, then disappears into the kitchen. Shortly afterwards Nina hears the hum of a coffee grinder.

I decided to take retirement, she says upon her return. She sets out a small plate of Italian *cantuccini* and two ceramic mugs then sits on the grey wool sofa opposite Nina. She wears her silver hair with dignity, loose down to her shoulders. Her soft, stylish clothing oozes quality.

I'd been teaching Norwegian at the teacher-training college ever since I graduated. I was bored.

Nina nods.

Toralf gave up work three years ago.

Did he work at the teacher-training college too?

Yes, Sigrid says, in the music department.

I see.

But you're still planning on working for a while longer?

I think so, Nina says. I'll be sixty-two next year.

I was excited to see what the transition to retirement would be like, Sigrid says. But now... she begins, casting a bleak look in Ask's direction. Now we have our hands full all of a sudden.

She appears to be tackling the task with impressive warmth, to Nina's mind. Ask shuffles across the room and creeps over to his grandmother. She passes him a biscuit.

It must be something of an upheaval, Nina says, but hopefully it won't be forever—

Sigrid interrupts her.

At the same time, he fills some sort of void.

She flicks through a pile of papers from the box before stopping.

Void isn't quite right, she says. Mari's absence, it fills us to the brim. It's more that he demands so much of us that we don't have the time to really, properly think about how bloody awful the whole situation is, she says, and Nina is shocked by gentle Sigrid Nilsen's foray into mild profanity.

Sigrid gets up all of a sudden, goes into the kitchen and returns with the coffee pot. She pours some into each mug.

Do you have grandchildren?

A little girl, she's three, Nina says.

Living nearby?

Yes, she lives in Bergen too.

Lovely, Sigrid says. Grandchildren are such a gift.

Nina glances up and out of the window looking across the fjord.

It'll be wonderful for Ask to spend some time out here, she says. Playing with feathers instead of bumping his way around padded play equipment.

Sigrid smiles meekly.

Mari, does she have any siblings? Nina asks cautiously.

No, Sigrid replies. But Toralf and I are still fit and well, and we've got the space, she says, understanding the subtext to Nina's question.

Yes, Nina says, a little too eagerly, trying to demonstrate her full agreement.

Sigrid Nilsen comes across as cool and composed, just as one might when fear and dread take hold. It's too soon for tears, or too late, perhaps. The way forward for now calls for calmly spoken words and the controlled, synchronised movement of one's head and hands and arms and feet, anything and everything to prevent one from tumbling over the edge.

We were there on Sunday just two weeks ago, she says. It was Ask's third birthday. Everything was so normal. I... She stops and lowers her gaze.

We did all the same things as usual, she says. We went for a walk, Mari had baked a cake, there was nothing to suggest anything was awry.

Nina swallows. She and Ingeborg had been there the day after Ask's birthday.

We talked about Christmas, Sigrid says, looking up. She wanted to have us over there, to arrange everything; she'd never done it before. Christmas dinner with all the trimmings, salted and dried mutton ribs, mashed swede and potatoes, aquavit, rice pudding, the works. We didn't waste any time accepting.

Sounds lovely, Nina says, responding on autopilot before remembering that plans had been forced to change.

Sigrid Nilsen shows no emotion. She continues to leaf through the stack of paper, turning each one over and holding it up to the light, as if she were looking for prints or evidence of something suspicious, and carries on talking.

But then she turned up here, just a few days later. Wednesday. She called from the ferry and told us she was on her way, she and Ask, both of them on the bus. Completely out of the blue. Toralf drove up the road to collect them, she had all these bags with her. There's always a certain degree of stuff you're required to haul around with you when you go somewhere with a child in tow, but still. Two large bags, enough clothing to last several weeks.

Nina swallows.

Finally moving back home? Toralf joked. We didn't realise at that point that she'd been thrown out.

Nina opens her mouth to explain, but Sigrid Nilsen carries on. She asked if she could stay with us until she came up with some sort of solution, she says without looking at Nina. Obviously we agreed.

She wasn't actually thrown out... Nina begins, but Sigrid pays no attention to her interjection.

The rest of her things are in a storage unit in Fyllingsdalen, she says. The police have been through everything, of course, but they haven't found anything of interest.

No? What about her phone, computer?

She left both here. The police have searched it all. Nothing, Sigrid says, shaking her head. It all gives the impression that she almost purposefully withdrew from life, bit by bit, she says steadily, gazing into the middle distance. As if she's ceased to exist, slowly but surely over time. She sidelined any friends and social life and work commitments … In the end, Ask was all she had left.

But she *did* have a job, Nina objects.

She went from being a soloist with some of the world's finest symphony orchestras to proofreading pamphlets, Sigrid responds dryly. Oh, I don't know.

What happened after she arrived? Nina asks.

Toralf made the beds up for them and I put Ask to sleep. Mari sat at the computer and searched for flats, sent emails, called people. She's always been a problem-solver. But there's not a great deal of choice on such a modest income. Later that evening she needed to take a break. We had something to eat, opened a bottle of wine. She was very resigned about the whole thing, Sigrid says, and now she's looking up at Nina once again, no hint of blame in her eyes.

Ask slides off the sofa and shuffles back over to his toys, all seemingly hand-picked by Sigrid: wooden puzzles and building blocks, and a stack of classic children's books.

We suggested that she didn't necessarily need to look at places in Bergen, Sigrid says. Perhaps she could simply move out here. Not living under our roof on a permanent basis, obviously, but just until something more suitable cropped up here on the island. That would make a lot more sense than finding somewhere in Bergen, plus she'd always have babysitters she could call upon. That way she could even go back out on tour.

And what did she have to say to that?

She didn't even want to talk about it at first, but we saw her beginning to entertain the idea. She had this air of resigned optimism about her.

And what about her job?

She could do her work for the publisher from anywhere.

So why did she move to Bergen in the first place? Nina asks.

Sigrid looks at her, seemingly puzzled as to why she's so interested. In the silence that descends, they hear Ask humming to himself, and Nina recognises one of Grieg's Lyric Pieces as Ask attempts to fit two puzzle pieces together.

Things broke down between her and her husband, she says eventually, her tone curt. It wasn't pretty. She seemed to feel the need to start afresh somewhere new.

Surely it would have made more sense for her husband to move away? Nina says.

Why?

Wasn't it he who left her?

You seem to know an awful lot about this, Sigrid remarks.

I— Nina begins, but Sigrid interrupts her.

It was a little more complicated than that. As I say, she wanted to get away.

All of a sudden she brings her palms down, slapping her thighs lightly before standing up.

Now then, Ask, shall we have a little nap in the buggy?

Ask looks up from his jigsaw puzzle. The clock shows twelve.

He dropped his daytime naps a while back, but after all that's happened... she begins ruefully. She leads him downstairs and Nina gets up and follows them.

I won't keep you, Nina says.

No, no, Sigrid says. She gets down on her knees and wraps the boy up in a thick, warm, wool suit before pulling a cosy-looking hat down over his ears.

I'm just going to pop him in the buggy. You can join us, if you like.

Ask drifts off just a few metres down the path, which follows the water's edge before curving around and up on the other side of the college.

See that, she says to Nina. He just needs to recharge his batteries.

They walk for a while without speaking in order to avoid waking the boy.

I met Niklas Bull, Nina says eventually.

Sigrid stops in her tracks and looks at her.

Because of the box, Nina says quickly. He was the one who passed me your names.

Did you speak to him on the phone, or did you actually meet him? she asks.

He's in Bergen now, Nina says. I met him, very briefly.

Sigrid starts walking again.

And? she asks.

And what?

What did he say?

He said he hadn't seen her in over three years.

Yes, Sigrid replies tensely. That figures.

Other than that, he said very little. It was only a brief meeting.

Sigrid is silent.

Do you know why they split? Nina asks eventually.

No, Sigrid says, and doesn't seem interested in going into further detail.

But they lived here for a few years?

When they returned from Germany, Sigrid says. Four years ago now.

That's young these days, Nina says. For a woman, I mean, wanting to start a family in her mid-twenties.

Start a family? Sigrid says, looking at her.

Wasn't that their reason for moving here?

No, Sigrid says. Absolutely not. My mother died. She had a house in Ås, which we let them rent for almost nothing. They thought it made for a nice base. You could get to Oslo fairly quickly and out into the wider world from there, there are flights twice daily. The house was sold a while back, of course.

So she didn't want to quit music?

Not at all, Sigrid says. To throw away ten, fifteen years' worth of training? She's been a professional musician since she was a teenager, it's her whole life, not the kind of thing you just stop doing.

But hard with a young child to think about, perhaps, Nina says.

That's right, Sigrid says, falling quiet.

They walk in silence for a while along the wet gravel path. The track is flanked by dense holly until the landscape opens up around them and they catch sight of the fjord. Beside the path is a lone bench.

We had an argument, a big one, Sigrid says, stopping in her tracks.

An argument?

The day after, she says, pushing the brake on the buggy with her foot.

The day she disappeared. She had spent all morning on the computer looking for places here on the island. Toralf and I were down here by the water with Ask. By the time we got home, she'd found somewhere that might actually work. She and Toralf even drove out to have a look at it. It wasn't a viewing; they just had a look from outside. By the time they returned, she was excited. The house itself was small, cosy, inexpensive, and it seemed to be in good condition. It even had a small garden.

And she would have been able to secure a mortgage?

Properties here don't cost what they do in Bergen, Sigrid says, taking a seat on the bench.

No, obviously, Nina says, but still. A single mother on a modest income.

She sold her violins, Sigrid says tersely.

Oh, Nina says, sitting down beside her.

That was the reason for our argument. We were ready to help her out financially if she moved out here, but she refused, said she didn't need help. Because she'd sold her violins, she said. It was exactly as I'd feared. Twenty years of intensive training, costly study, all cast aside, just like that. I couldn't hide my disappointment.

Her eyes are shining.

And then I was stupid enough to tell her that the money was ours. We'd helped her throughout her career and had never received a penny for any of it. We'd driven her here, there and everywhere, arranged lessons, travelled the world with her, we'd done everything you could possibly imagine...

Sigrid stops, composes herself.

In reality, Toralf sacrificed much of his career to travel with her all around Europe, she says eventually. He taught music at the college. The two of them spent years on the road, right up until she was old enough to go by herself.

Slowly she shakes her head.

What did she say when you said that?

She wanted to take Ask back to Bergen at once. She started packing. But where in Bergen? I asked, where are you going to live? Sounding somewhat triumphant, I'm sure. I should have been more mature about it. Toralf was our go-between, he's the family mediator. He asked me to step back. I took the car and drove to the shops. By the time I returned, she'd gone.

Gone?

She wanted to go out. Walk off her anger while Toralf put Ask to bed.

And that was the last time?

That was the last time.

She stares into the distance, teary-eyed.

She still hadn't appeared by the time the evening news had finished. Ask was fast asleep, she would never stay out for so long without letting us know. And she'd left her phone here. Toralf drove out to look for her. He took a torch; it was pitch-black out there. He walked the paths we knew she usually took, but she was nowhere to be seen. He got back around one.

Nothing? Nina asks, even though she knows the answer.

He wanted to call the police at that point. I persuaded him to wait, she says, falling silent. I was so sure that she was just trying to punish me.

You couldn't have known— Nina begins, but she is interrupted by a piercing ringtone. Sigrid quickly plunges her hand into her pocket and silences the ringing to keep Ask from waking.

Toralf, she says, looking up from the screen. She takes a few steps away and speaks in hushed tones as Nina gazes out at the snow-covered mountains across the fjord.

Sigrid returns and places the phone down on the bench.

I need to get back, she says. I've got to let an electrician in.

She shakes her head.

I'm always forgetting things, Sigrid says. Just forgetting everything, all the time.

That's not all that strange, really, Nina says. It's a difficult time.

Sigrid takes the brake off the buggy and looks at Nina inquisitively.

We've got a cabin in Oldervik, Nina says, nodding in the opposite direction. My car's up there. So, I think I'll leave you here.

Thanks for coming, Sigrid says.

I really do hope everything works out, Nina says.

Thank you, Sigrid says, no trace of hope in her tone, thank you for that.

She turns around and pushes the buggy ahead of her, walking quickly along the path, the salty breeze blowing through her hair.

Nina is just about to make her way back to the car when she

sees Sigrid's mobile phone on the bench. She opens her mouth to call after her, but stops. Sigrid has disappeared around a corner. She picks up the phone and slowly follows, pressing the home button: it's unlocked.

Her pulse racing, her gaze fixed on the path ahead, she opens the messages app and quickly searches for Mari's name, half an eye on the path in case Sigrid has turned around to come back for it.

There's only one message there. It's three years old.

*Say hello to Ask*, she reads. *3,150 grams and 50cm. He arrived at midnight, Mum and baby both doing well. Love from Mari.*

She closes the message quickly and jogs along the path until she catches sight of Sigrid Nilsen in the distance.

Sigrid! she shouts.

It's raining across the fjord. Nina drives slowly off the ferry at Halhjem, it's only early afternoon but darkness surrounds her. The sky is leaden, the way you only ever see it on the west coast in December. The knowledge that things won't start to look up until April. The car headlights in the long queue sparkle red and yellow against the shiny black tarmac.

Her stomach flips whenever she thinks about the way she and Ingeborg turned up and practically hounded Mari Nilsen out of her home, a weary and possibly depressed single mother.

She was probably already out of sorts. But what if their visit was the final straw?

Or did the argument with Sigrid trigger something? Nina wonders to herself, feeling a sense of relief creep over her at the mere thought.

Her phone vibrates on the centre console, Kaia's name lights up against the dark background of the screen.

Where are you? she asks.

Are we supposed to be meeting up? Nina asks, surprised.

No, I just meant in general, Kaia says.

Things have been busy, I'm just on my way back from Tornøy.

In the middle of the week? Why's that?

What are you doing tomorrow evening? Nina asks her, thinking that it might be good to include Kaia in the mysterious disappearance of Mari Nilsen.

Nothing.

I've got tickets for Grieg Hall. The opera.

Opera? Kaia replies with surprise. Which one?

*Bluebeard's Castle.*

Isn't that for children? Kaia replies sceptically, and all of a sudden Nina is unsure.

I don't know. It starts at 8pm, I don't imagine it's for children.

Who knows, Kaia says. Shall we meet in the bar an hour before it's due to start?

She can see a light at the upstairs window as she parks up outside the house. Mads is home. He opens his office door as she climbs the stairs.

Where have you been?

What do you mean?

I popped by your office today, he says, following her into the kitchen. But it was empty.

I was over on Tornøy, she says, placing her bag on the worktop. I told you I'd need the car.

On Tornøy?

I had a meeting, she says, she feels uncomfortable about explaining that she's been to see Mari Nilsen's parents.

Well, nobody in the department knew where you were, Mads says accusatorily.

They're probably as good at listening as you are. What did you need?

My seminar was cancelled, I was hoping to take you out to lunch.

Bad luck, Nina says. Maybe I can make it up to you with a frozen pizza?

Shortly afterwards they find themselves sitting at the dining table, each with a cardboard-like slice of pizza and a bottle of sparkling water as they stare at their laptop screens.

Nina follows her new routine: after confirming that there haven't been any updates on the Mari Nilsen case, she opens the property pages and checks to see if her search criteria, which have been somewhat watered down over time, have turned up any new results. She's become accustomed to seeing both the investigation and the house hunt treading water, but she adjusts the price range on her property search, lowering it this time, and her heart leaps when she discovers a traditional house on Strangehagen.

Take a look at this, she says.

You're getting desperate, he says after having a brief look at the ad.

We need to broaden our horizons, she says bravely.

What, and live in a crooked, creaky, three-hundred-year-old house on a bustling tourist trail?

It's got soul of sorts, she objects.

Mads clears the table, taking the half-eaten pizza to the kitchen and disposing of the leftovers.

There's a viewing on Saturday morning, she calls after him.

I'd think again on that one, Mads replies, filling the coffee machine with water.

I was at Mari Nilsen's mother's house today, she says all of a sudden as he returns to the room and takes a seat. While I was over on Tornøy.

Oh? You two know each other?

We were at college together forty years ago, as it happens, but I don't know her, as such. Ingeborg found a box of Mari's things in the basement.

The police hadn't taken it away?

Obviously not. But it was just old transcripts and the like, nothing very exciting. All the same, I thought her parents ought to have it. They've got a three-year-old on their hands now, she adds.

How awful, he says, shaking his head. Not looking after their grandchild, obviously, but the fact their daughter is gone.

I know what you mean.

What did they say, did they know anything?

Nothing at all. But I got the sense that... She stops.

That what?

She and her mother had argued, she said. That was the last thing that had happened before her disappearance. And... she begins.

And what?

I don't think they had the best relationship.

Aha, so you two have something in common, then, Mads says, but Nina shakes her head.

No, she says. It was worse than that. I don't think they had much contact at all.

But wasn't she visiting them when she went missing?

That's right, she replies pensively.

He looks at her before getting up to deal with the coffee.

I'm off to Grieg Hall with Kaia tomorrow evening, she says.

*You're* going to Grieg Hall? And no one's twisting your arm? he asks, pouring them both a cup. That's a new one. What's on?

Bartók, she replies quickly.

I see, he says. Which one?

I'm not sure. It's an opera.

Are you going to see *Bluebeard's Castle*? he asks with surprise.

How did you know that?

Nina, he says, cocking his head to one side, it's Bartók's only opera. Everybody knows that.

This is embarrassing, she says. But...

But what?

Mari Nilsen's ex-husband is the conductor.

Mads breaks into laughter, and Nina feels herself blush, the redness rising up her throat.

That explains it. You're taking this private-investigator stuff seriously, aren't you?

# Thursday 6th December

Kaia is already sitting at a table as she climbs the stairs to the bar on the first floor. She raises her glass with an ironically polite nod and crosses her legs. Nina buys a drink at the bar and takes a seat across from her sister-in-law.

So, Kaia says, what's new on the house front?

Not a thing, Nina replies.

Nothing? she says. But you're viewing places, surely?

Nina shakes her head.

There's nothing to view.

Don't blame the housing market, Kaia says. It's your lack of willingness to accept the situation that's the real problem here.

Thank you for that, Nina says. Is this what people pay you for?

Don't worry about it, Kaia says, waving a hand, I'll bill you later. But what *are* you doing, if not viewing houses? I haven't heard a peep out of you since our weekend in Oldervik.

Nina glances discreetly around the foyer and leans in slightly.

You know we've got that terrace house on Birkeveien, the one that Mads and Jo inherited from their aunt? The one we rented out? Ingeborg and Eirik are moving into it.

Are they?

And I don't know if you've seen in the newspapers about the young woman who's gone missing?

The violinist, Kaia says. Yes, I saw that.

You know her?

We've been to several of her concerts, Kaia nods. Mari Bull, wasn't it, something like that?

Yes, or Mari Nilsen, as she's now known. She's the person we've been renting the house to.

You what? Kaia says, wide-eyed.

It's strange, Nina says. Ingeborg and I met her three days before she went missing. Ingeborg was so desperate to see the house, Nina says, looking around. The tables surrounding them have suddenly filled up with grey-haired, well-dressed audience members their own age and above.

Nina lowers her voice: I'm afraid that we might have, I don't know, set something in motion. Ingeborg was awful, to be quite honest with you, and within two days Mari Nilsen had moved out.

Moved out? Kaia says.

She packed up and—

Disappeared?

First she went back to her parents' house. Then she was supposed to be taking a walk in the neighbourhood, and ... *poof.*

Kaia shakes her head in astonishment.

But surely there isn't any connection, she says.

She's got a three-year-old son, too, Nina adds. Who's now living with his grandparents on Tornøy while his mother is missing.

My God, Kaia says.

But here's the thing, Nina says. Niklas Bull, the new conductor here this evening, he was married to Mari Nilsen.

Really? Kaia says, leaning back and bringing her glass to her lips.

And I met him a few days ago. She'd left a box behind at the house. I got in touch with him to try to find out her parents' names, so I could hand it over—

A box? You didn't take it to the police?

The contents weren't anything special, Nina says, sounding vexed. Anyway, that's not the point. When he heard that I'd been renting the house to her, he wanted to meet me.

She leans across the table.

He walked out on Mari Nilsen when she was pregnant, she whispers, and Kaia raises her eyebrows. But now he's come to the city to win her back. They were supposed to meet the day she disappeared—

At that moment the bell rings, and the two of them drink up and follow the crowd making its way into the concert hall.

Their seats aren't the best. They're in row thirteen, a good way away from the stage, Kaia sitting directly behind an enormous man wearing a hat, who dominates most of her view. She leans in and pretends to whip the hat off in one swift, smooth motion to a ripple of restrained laughter through the row behind them. It soon becomes clear that Nina's own view of the podium on which Niklas Bull stands is good, which is the most important thing.

The hum of small talk from the audience and the atmosphere among the orchestra merges and rises upwards, and Nina realises that this has always been what she's liked most about being here: the sound of instruments being tuned, the moments before the performance begins, before the conductor steps onto the podium and lifts his baton. In those instants, your expectations remain intact; the tuning of the instruments is like the prelude to a climax, but when the orchestra begins to play, everything swiftly goes downhill.

Almost simultaneously, the tuning and the hum of the audience stops, and a moment later, the new principal conductor emerges from the left of the stage dressed in a fitted black suit. He hurries to his spot with a proud expression on his face and brings the entire orchestra to its feet with the sweep of one hand before greeting the first violinist and taking to the podium with a spring in his step. He gives the audience a deep bow with a wide smile before his face appears to fall, and he turns around quickly to face his orchestra.

Nina catches sight of the same thing he has: the empty seat in the middle of the fifth row.

He lifts his baton, and menacing notes rise from the orchestra, like something straight out of a fairy tale. At the same time, two opera singers take to the stage and stand on either side of the conductor.

For well over an hour, the soloists, the orchestra and the conductor dominate proceedings. Judging by the rise and fall between raucous and more subdued moments, a dramatic story is unfolding before them, but Nina is unable to understand a single syllable of the foreign-language performance and simply sits there, trapped within her own frustration.

As the final quivering tones ebb away following a powerful climax, she feels relief sweep over her.

Niklas Bull lowers his baton, turns around and gives a deep bow to the sound of applause and stamping feet throughout the concert hall, even from the thirteenth row. Nina can see his cheeks glistening with tears.

He hurries off stage and disappears.

I feel like I've been duped, Kaia says afterwards as they follow the wave of audience members making their way through Grieg Hall and out into the wet December chill. They call it an opera, but the stage setting was non-existent! *Bluebeard's Castle* without the castle!

Well, the music was good, at any rate, Nina says, pulling on a pair of leather gloves. Fancy something to eat?

They huddle together against the cold and make their way along Lille Lungegårdsvann to Skostredet, slipping into the tiny, warm *enoteca*.

The owner nods appreciatively and immediately makes his way around the bar, taking their coats and showing them to a table in the furthest corner. It's dark and busy, candles line the walls and light up the tables, middle-aged women in pairs speaking in hushed tones all around them, others just like them, she gives a university colleague a brief nod.

You hadn't actually finished your story about this conductor, Kaia reminds her. So, they were supposed to meet up on the day she disappeared?

Nina nods.

Ingeborg even bumped into him at the house on Birkeveien, so he was telling the truth about that.

Is there something he's *not* telling the truth about, in your opinion?

What do I know? But it *is* something of a coincidence, Nina says, scanning the board above the bar, where wine recommendations have been scrawled.

That's why it would have been interesting to know what the opera was actually about.

How do you mean?

He told me that this debut concert was intended as a nod to Mari Nilsen.

Kaia almost jumps out of her chair.

What? Nina asks.

*Bluebeard's Castle*? A nod to his ex-wife, his *missing* ex-wife? Kaia says.

Did you read up on it in advance?

Of course I did, Kaia says. I'm a sophisticated individual, after all. You must be familiar with the story of *Bluebeard's Castle*?

No.

You haven't heard the folktale about Captain Bluebeard? Kaia says, dumbfounded. What kind of professor of literature *are* you?

I'm exactly that, a professor of literature, Nina says with a snort, *not* a professor of folklore.

And what with you having had such success with Milja lately, too. You'll need to save the tale of Captain Bluebeard for when she's proving particularly challenging, Kaia says.

Come on, spill the beans, Nina says impatiently.

Finally my undergraduate studies on Bettelheim are paying off.

Bethlehem?

Bruno Bettelheim, Kaia says. A scandalous figure in the world of psychology inspired by Freud. He took his own life at the age of eighty-six.

Better late than never.

The owner appears by their table and asks what they'd like. Nina asks him to bring some antipasti and a nice wine to pair with it in order to get rid of him.

Bettelheim used fairy tales in his treatment of psychotic children, Kaia says. The symbolic language of fairy tales speaks to the subconscious and illustrates common inner conflicts. Sibling jealousy, fear of not being loved by one's parents, and so on. Hansel and Gretel, for instance, sent out into the forest by their own parents...

Nina drums her nails against the tabletop with impatience.

... buuuut back to Captain Bluebeard, Kaia says. I just had to jog my memory there. Captain Bluebeard is a nobleman with a frightful blue beard. He's been married numerous times, but now he's once again on the hunt for a new wife, and he hears in the village of a woman with two wonderful young daughters.

One of whom is soon to have her life turned upside down?

They think he's awful, but still they accept his invitation to visit one of his country estates, along with a number of their friends and young gentlemen. Once there, they have such a charming time that the youngest daughter returns home only to declare: well, his beard isn't all *that* blue...!

Oh dear, Nina says.

And so there follows a wedding. The girl moves in. Shortly afterwards, Bluebeard goes travelling. He gives his young wife two keys. One is a universal key, which she can use as she pleases. The other – Kaia says, lowering her voice and leaning across the table in such a way that the candlelight flickers across her face – the other is a perfectly innocent-looking little key, designed to fit the lock of a small door at the very end of a long corridor on the ground floor. But she is strictly forbidden to open the door. If you do so, Bluebeard tells her, my fury will know no bounds. And he proceeds to hop in his carriage and leave.

Hmm, Nina says. And perhaps the prospect of using the little key becomes too tempting to ignore?

Perhaps? Kaia says. The girl invites her friends to visit, and they open all the other doors in the house, doors to rooms filled with gold and jewels, glorious textiles, lavish items of furniture, you can imagine. But as her friends revel in Bluebeard's unparalleled riches, the girl is gripped by ever-increasing curiosity.

What could be hiding behind the tiny door at the end of the corridor? Nina says.

Yes, what could it possibly be? Eventually she opens the door. Unfortunately it's so dark inside that she can't see a thing. But after a while her eyes become accustomed to the darkness, and she discovers that the floor is wet with blood. Reflected in that blood are several women, hanging on hooks along the wall, women whose throats were cut by Bluebeard himself.

Yikes, Nina says, genuinely surprised at the turn of events.

In her confusion, the girl drops the key and it, too, ends up covered in blood—

The restaurant owner returns carrying a large platter of cheese, ham and olives, oil, bread and two glasses of Tuscan wine.

And then the nobleman returns home, I'm guessing? Nina suggests, thanking the owner with a nod.

Yes, can you imagine? And has she washed the blood off the key? Nope. No matter how diligently she scrubs it, whenever she's managed to clean one side, she finds just as much blood on the other.

She clearly hasn't tried ammonia and washing-up liquid, Nina remarks.

Bluebeard is less than pleased to discover that his brand-new bride has overstepped the one and only mark he set for her. And so she must pay with her life, just like the others, the wives that came before her.

Here's a suggestion for a double date, Nina says, dipping her bread in oil: Bluebeard and the girl, plus Henry VIII and Anne Boleyn.

That would certainly be something. But the folktale takes a less sombre turn: the girl's two brothers save her at the last minute and kill Bluebeard. And since they were married, the girl inherits his many riches and finds a slightly more ordinary chap to marry.

And what exactly does Bettelheim think these psychotic children might draw from this, dare I ask?

Kaia samples the wine, shaking her head.

No idea. I'll need to dig out my old essays on the subject.

No need for that, Nina says. But the fact that Niklas Bull chose that particular piece as a nod to his ex-wife, that seems slightly warped, wouldn't you say?

They fall silent.

But the opera, Kaia says slowly, it differs from the folktale in a few ways.

Oh? Nina says.

In the opera, there are seven keys, not two. Seven doors. And the ending is very different. You'll need to read it for yourself. I can't remember all the details. You'll find it online somewhere.

Kaia pops an olive in her mouth.

But Bettelheim... she continues, taking a sip before setting her glass down and leaning back in her chair. She closes her eyes, as she tends to when she's in lecture mode. He's just one of many interpreters of such fairy tales. There are a whole host of traditions when it comes to extracting meaning from folktales, she begins, and Nina does her best to suppress the desire to pull out her phone and start researching the opera.

Is Bluebeard simply intended as a warning to young women not to marry a man with a dubious past and, eh, a blue beard? Kaia asks rhetorically. Or what about Charles Perrault's take on the subject, for instance? He published the tale for the very first time, you know, in the same collection as *Little Red Riding Hood*, *Puss in Boots*, *Cinderella*—

And he said what, exactly?

Well, he concluded the tale of Captain Bluebeard by writing: 'Curiosity, in spite of its appeal, often leads to deep regret.'

A classic case of victim blaming, Nina replies dryly.

But a feminist interpretation would claim that Bluebeard is a tale of violence in the home, pure and simple, and the man's unending abuse of the woman. A Jungian take would assert that Bluebeard represents something within us all: an innate predator that you must learn to rein in if you are ever to develop a healthy relationship with your true self.

Nina signals the owner to top up their glasses and he quickly fetches a bottle from the shelf behind him.

A Lacanian interpretation, on the other hand, Kaia says, and her stream of words is momentarily drowned out by the gurgle of the bottle. She thanks the owner. A Lacanian interpretation would take a more in-depth look at the relationship of power and the act of denying others access to knowledge. Can you imagine Mads saying that to you, for instance, hm? 'Here you go, have this key, but it won't end well for you if you decide to use it!'

Not exactly a recipe for a healthy marriage, no, Nina says.

Bluebeard's handing over of the key is a test of trust. And the women fail that test, one by one.

It seems to me Bluebeard is hoping that's exactly what will happen, Nina says, it provides him with an excuse to do away with them in good conscience.

There's something in that. But anyway, last but not least: the Freudian interpretation of *Bluebeard's Castle*, Kaia says, opening her hands like a lid of a box, but as she does so the bell above the door rings, and Nina ducks instinctively. Kaia gives her a strange look before turning discreetly to look over at the restaurant door, where three men and one woman have entered. They take off their coats and hang them on the coat stand, chatting as they are shown to a table in a separate room.

Nina sits with her back to Niklas Bull as he passes her, doing her best to pretend that nothing is amiss. Once the small group is out of sight, she leans in towards Nina and mimes without a sound: *Was that him?* Nina nods and indicates that they ought to radically change the subject under discussion.

What about castles, Kaia says, any nice castles on the market these days?

On her way back from the toilet, she feels his gaze fall upon her. She stops in her tracks when she hears him say her name.

It's Nina, isn't it? he says.

You've got a good memory, she says.

He gets up. The three others, musicians from the orchestra, she assumes, look up at her, half interested.

Congratulations on your debut performance, she says.

Were you there? he asks, surprised.

I do my best to get along there when I can, she says. It was a wonderful performance.

Thank you, Niklas says as the others smile faintly in her direction. It felt good to get it over and done with. Won't you take a seat?

Thank you, she says, but I'll leave you all in peace. I'm sitting just out there.

He makes his way around the table and approaches her, taking her to one side, over towards the toilets.

Did you manage to hand over the box? he whispers.

I was there just yesterday.

Really? What did they say? Did they know anything?

No, she replies. Not that Sigrid told me, anyway.

And what about Toralf, was he there?

Briefly, he left when I arrived.

That's a shame, he says.

What makes you say that?

Mari and Sigrid, he says, shaking his head. Not the best of friends.

Electra complex? she says, and he looks at her with a curious expression.

Don't mind me, she says. Just a joke. I'm sorry. She's taking good care of Ask, in any case.

That's good to hear, he replies.

He's well, she says with emphasis, looking at Niklas, but he just nods.

That's good to hear, he repeats, indifferent to the fact that she's brought his son into the conversation.

The police have no leads, she says.

My God, he says, running a hand through his curls.

What if she doesn't turn up? Nina asks. There must be something criminal at play, in such a case. She can't simply have walked out on her own son.

He says nothing, simply shaking his head with his eyes closed.

What do you think? she asks, the words slipping out before she can stop them. Is Ask going to grow up with his grandparents?

He looks at her inquisitively.

Or with his father? she continues, her tone is more strident than she'd realised.

He looks at her in puzzlement for a moment before taking her by the arm and leading her to a small table in the narrow passageway.

You have to forgive my directness, she says, slightly afraid all of a sudden, taking a seat. But Ask— she whispers, before they are suddenly interrupted.

There you are, a voice says. They look up, and there stands Kaia, wearing a somewhat cheerfully bitter expression.

I was just on my way back over, Nina says, waving her away with a hand before Kaia makes a move to sit down with them.

My goodness, Kaia says in a feigned tone, isn't this the conductor?

Niklas Bull nods.

I didn't realise you two knew each other, she says to Nina with a somewhat theatrical smile.

Have you worked your way through the entire wine cellar? Nina asks.

Kaia looks around for a free chair.

I'll be right over, Nina repeats through gritted teeth, nodding in the direction of their table.

OK, Kaia says, somewhat indignant, turning around and returning to their table.

Nina turns back around to face Niklas Bull.

You were saying?

He brings his glass to his lips to take a sip.

You know that we moved from Germany to Tornøy?

Nina nods.

We'd both managed to establish ourselves on the European scene, we had promising careers ahead of us. But Mari spoke more and more of moving home. And after many years travelling, it was nice to finally settle in one place, in some sense.

And practical to have grandparents nearby, Nina interjects.

Niklas Bull shakes his head firmly.

No, he says. We didn't have any plans for children at that stage. It was too early for all that.

So, Ask was an accident, Nina says.

He erupts in dark laughter.

She looks at him, puzzled.

I'm sorry, he says, batting his laughter away with one hand before rubbing his face.

I don't quite know what to call it, he says with a roguish expression.

What do you mean?

Mari had an accident, but not with me.

Ask isn't yours? she whispers.

Slowly he shakes his head.

That was the reason. For our split.

You're certain? she asks.

It wasn't a complicated mathematical puzzle to solve, he says, cocking his head to one side. I was the visiting conductor for the BBC Philharmonic for over a month at the time she fell pregnant.

Gosh, she says.

We separated. Shortly after that she moved to Bergen. I got a job in Oslo. We didn't have much contact after that.

So you were the conductor for the Oslo Philharmonic? she asks, her tone sufficiently curious to avoid giving away the fact that she's already researched him thoroughly, and he nods.

But as I say, we'd started writing to each other, he says. Over the past few months.

Yes, how did that come about?

Her father and I had kept in touch over the past few years. He was as upset as I was when Mari and I split up. Mari struggled in the years that followed. I think Toralf saw how good I'd been for her, in spite of everything.

Struggled how?

Things hadn't exactly turned out how she thought they might. She had a bright future ahead of her as far as her career was concerned, she'd worked towards it from the age of five. Now she's a single mother, and music plays no part in her life. The thing she once lived for has been lost.

Perhaps she lives for her life as a mother, Nina objects, but Niklas Bull ignores her.

It was Toralf who tipped me off about the former conductor stepping down. He has his contacts on the scene. So, I wrote to Mari to ask her how she might feel about me walking the same city streets.

And?

We agreed to ... well, to try, basically. To take things slowly, meet up first, but, between the lines, to see if, in time, we might be able to find our way back to one another.

He pauses, takes a long swig of his beer.

Obviously it was a huge shock, the fact she was pregnant with someone else's child, he says eventually. Completely surreal. But when I moved to Oslo and gained some distance, I started to re-evaluate things. Started to think that yes, yes, it *had* been a huge betrayal, but we'd both wanted children in the long run. And now she had one. When we re-established contact, I made it clear that I wanted to be a father, if she'd let me. I wanted to treat Ask as if he were my own.

Yes?

I don't know anything about the biological father, about what kind of contact they have. I just know that they're not in any sort of relationship. She was very clear about that fact.

Nina cranes her neck from where she's sitting by the wall and casts a glance in the direction of the bar. Kaia has struck up conversation with a few others, she'll cope on her own for a little longer.

But you must have had a few problems in advance of … the pregnancy? she asks warily.

He hesitates slightly.

I was working a lot, he says. And Mari was unwell for a while.

Unwell?

She recovered, but it put her out of play for a while, quite literally. She pottered around the new house, but the job offers that came my way proved to be too much of a temptation to refuse.

He shrugs.

I don't know. Maybe it was a mistake moving out there.

He gets up quickly.

Anyway, I won't waste any more of your time, he says.

You've done nothing of the sort, she replies, also getting up.

You will let me know if you hear anything? he says.

Yes, she says. I will.

He returns to his table and she returns to Kaia, who is once again sitting on her own. She looks at Nina with an expression of feigned offence.

Shall we have another glass of something? Nina asks, apologetically.

She waves over the owner of the restaurant, who immediately appears to top up their glasses.

So, did he have anything interesting to divulge? Kaia asks, but just as Nina opens her mouth to reply, Kaia stops her with a hand.

Before you say anything, I just have to finish up what I was saying before, Kaia says. The Freudian interpretation of *Bluebeard*, if you remember? It won't surprise you to learn that it's all about sexuality.

No surprise at all, Nina says.

The man's rage at having been betrayed, to be more precise, Kaia says, raising her glass in Nina's direction.

## Saturday 8th December

How was it at Grieg Hall the day before yesterday, by the way? Mads asks, following her up the creaking staircase to the top floor.

She shrugs.

Let's just say that it wasn't like any opera I've ever seen. There were just two people standing there, singing.

No castles? No doors, no keys? Mads says, feigning shock on her behalf.

You don't exactly feel swept away by the story when the whole thing is in Czech, she grumbles.

Hungarian, Mads says, correcting her. And you *are* allowed to read up on it in advance, you know.

*Well*, Nina says, I decided to read up afterwards instead.

Oh?

She glances downstairs discreetly then leans in towards her husband. She lowers her voice.

I met Niklas Bull, she says under her breath. The ex-husband.

Yes, you said.

And he told me that *Bluebeard's Castle* was intended as his *nod* to Mari Nilsen...!

Mads casts a quizzical look in her direction.

So?

Are you familiar with the opera?

Not on a plot level, no, Mads says.

No, OK. Well, it's not exactly a typical declaration of love. Maybe that's what he was getting at. Or perhaps the idea was to scare her.

To scare her? Mads says.

Given that we know she's actually *missing*, Nina says, peering inside the bathroom. Alas, no bathtub.

That's not a deal-breaker for me, Mads says.

They make their way back down the slightly crooked staircase and step into the largest bedroom. The bed has been beautifully made, and there are elegant rosettes on the ceiling above.

But tell me, Mads says, how does the story go?

Well, she says, perching herself on the edge of the bed. There's Judith, that's her name, whose entire family is left weeping and wailing when she decides to shack up with the terrifying Bluebeard in his castle. In the darkness she can make out seven doors. Judith insists on letting some light in, but Bluebeard insinuates that there is good reason for his castle to be shrouded in darkness.

Mads sits down beside her.

The atmosphere between them is uncomfortable, to put it mildly, Nina continues. Judith reassures Bluebeard that she loves him, regardless of the secrets concealed behind those seven doors. Eventually, if not reluctantly, he hands over the key to the first door. The room behind it is revealed to be a blood-stained torture chamber.

Oh dear, Mads says.

Yes, not exactly a good sign. But on the other hand, a lord is surely within his rights to have a torture chamber.

Well, yes, in a sense.

But there still isn't enough light in the castle for Judith, so she is granted permission to open the second door. Behind it she finds a blood-spattered armoury.

Aha.

Behind the third door is an abundance of riches, and Judith is very taken by his many assets, even when she discovers that all of his gold is spattered with blood.

He doesn't seem too concerned with good hygiene, this Bluebeard, Mads says.

Nina stands up and walks over to the window.

You can see right into the neighbour's house from here, Nina says.

That goes both ways, Mads says.

They leave the bedroom and step into the main living area, where they sit at the dining table as the other people viewing the house pass by in a hum of conversation.

Behind the fourth door, Judith finds his secret garden – incredibly beautiful, but also blood-soaked. Every single lily and rose is speckled with the stuff. At this point Judith, finally somewhat suspicious, asks him the pressing question: 'Whose blood was shed in order that your garden might grow?'

And Bluebeard tells her...?

'Love me, ask no questions!'

This nod to Mari Nilsen is getting stranger by the minute.

The next door, let me think, Nina says, pondering the plot for a moment. Oh yes, it's a window looking out onto Bluebeard's realm. They both gaze out over the beautiful landscape together.

But?

Well, it's an unfortunate thing, she says, gesturing towards the window, but the clouds cast blood-red shadows—

Is everything alright here? a voice asks, and Mads and Nina both jump.

We're just admiring the view, Nina tells the agent, who nods and moves on.

I'm starting to see a pattern here, Mads says.

Perhaps so, but behind the sixth door is a beautiful little indoor lake. What's this mysterious body of water? Judith asks Bluebeard.

Let me guess, Mads says. Could it be *blood*?

Actually no, Nina says. It's tears.

Ah.

At this point, Bluebeard insists that the seventh door should remain locked forevermore.

But Judith isn't quite willing to agree to this, I imagine, Mads says, getting up.

Judith has finally had enough, Nina says. She accuses him of doing away with his first wives and watering his garden with their spilled blood.

Judith the Master Detective! Mads says.

'All those rumours about you!' Judith shouts at him indignantly, 'They were all true!'

That's rumours for you, Mads says. Plus, it's never a good sign when someone has been married *that* many times.

Ugh, Nina says, entering the kitchen. That's where us women always fall short, you know. Mimetic desire.

Mimetic what now?

We want what other women have. Gosh, has he really had *seven* wives? we think to ourselves. This Bluebeard must be quite the man!

They each perch on a bar stool.

Anyway. Judith is given the seventh key, Nina continues. Now it's Bluebeard who asks her to open the door. *Et voilà*, what do you imagine awaits them? His first three wives, alive and kicking.

Oh? Mads says, genuinely surprised.

But whether it's a life worth living is another story altogether. They stand there on show, each on some sort of podium, draped in beautiful flowing robes, all doing their best to balance heavy crowns on their heads. Bluebeard kneels before each of them, praising them one by one. And poor Judith...

Yes?

Judith grows jealous. My God, she says, looking up at them: I'm *nothing* compared to them.

You women really need to stop with all that comparison nonsense, Mads says. We like you just as you are.

Bluebeard sets to work dressing Judith up in the same elaborate robes and hanging enormous jewels around her neck as she begs him to stop. He places a giant crown on her head as Judith weeps. No, no, she says, it's far too heavy! But all she can do is teeter there, up on the podium, suffering in unbearable luxury alongside his other wives.

And that's that?

That's that.

Hmm, Mads says, gazing into thin air with an expression of wonder on his face. Hardly surprising that Mari Nilsen walked out, if you ask me.

He doesn't quite seem to be the perfect catch, no.

But do you really believe that he might have been involved in her disappearance? Mads asks.

She shakes her head, no idea.

She married young, Nina says. He must be ten years her senior. He obviously had the upper hand. She admired him, a renowned conductor, and she was a talented young woman herself, she felt chosen by him. And then she goes and falls pregnant by another man.

Quite some form of rebellion, Mads says.

He falls silent.

I think the police need to hear all this, he says eventually.

All what? she says.

This. The betrayal, the deception, Bluebeard.

She cocks her head to one side.

I have my doubts to what degree they'd consider a Bartók opera a red-hot lead, Nina says.

This is precisely the reason they need more literary scholars in the police force! Mads says.

Are you being serious?

Maybe you should get in touch with them. If you're lucky, you'll get talking to the right investigator.

I'm sure the child's father must live here, she says. It seems so decisive, the way she moved here when she was pregnant.

You don't think she was just trying to get away from Niklas Bull? Mads asks.

Or her parents, Nina says.

The agent glides into the kitchen in smart shoes polished to a high shine.

Lots of room for cooking up a storm in here, he says to Nina, beaming encouragingly and sweeping a hand across the kitchen.

Nina? Mads says with a snort. Chance would be a fine thing. That'll be me, I think you'll find.

The agent chuckles hesitantly and falls silent.

When was the house built? Nina asks in an attempt to sound pleasant.

1750, he chirps, and launches into detail about the very particular engravings on the bannisters.

Planning a career in museum curation now, are we? Mads whispers.

## Monday 10th December

In her sixty-one years on earth, she has never had a conversation with the police. She's never been the victim of a crime, has never witnessed anything of the sort, and has never been stopped for speeding, despite the fact that she routinely drives over the limit, particularly on the stretch between the ferry terminal at the north of Tornøy and Oldervik.

Now she finds herself being shown into the office of Detective Inspector Gro Vik. Vik is dressed in her uniform, with a simple ponytail at the nape of her neck, and wears a pair of rimless spectacles. She doesn't offer Nina a coffee. A clementine sits on her desk, which is otherwise perfectly neat and tidy.

She looks more like a school teacher than an investigator to Nina, who does all she can to smooth her cynically furrowed brow. Hardly surprising Mari Nilsen hasn't been found, she thinks to herself, before reprimanding herself for judging Vik based on her appearance and, if she's honest, the fact she's a woman.

I think you or one of your colleagues has already spoken to my husband, Nina begins after the detective takes down Nina's personal information.

Mads Glaser, Gro Vik says, looking up from a sheet of paper, something that causes Nina to think that she's already in the spotlight. I'll just set this to record, if that's OK with you? Vik says, and Nina nods.

Vik stares at Nina, waiting. Nina has been looking down her nose at the police force in recent weeks, the force that probably hasn't even managed to work out that the missing woman's ex-husband dedicated an opera about killing wives to her. But now, when the time comes to say the words out loud, she feels suddenly and excruciatingly aware of how ridiculous it all sounds.

Mari Nilsen was, I mean, *is*, our tenant, Nina says, fumbling, sensing just how suspiciously she's behaving as soon as she opens her mouth.

*Was* is surely correct, given that she gave notice a few days before her disappearance, isn't that right? Vik says, and Nina confirms this. Vik awaits further explanation with a neutral expression.

I didn't know her, Nina says, but I know her parents, loosely. I was in touch with them just recently, to...

She stops, suddenly painfully aware of the fact that she should have gone directly to the police with the box that Ingeborg found, rather than to Mari's parents.

...Express my sympathies, she says eventually, to let them know how sorry I was to hear that Mari is missing. She clears her throat, senses Vik's emotionless yet thoughtful gaze.

My husband and I, we're keen concert-goers, she continues, ashamed that a professor of literature should prove so incapable of producing even a vaguely coherent tale.

That's why I'm here, she concedes, and sees Vik raising an eyebrow ever so slightly in confusion.

As you know, Nina says, clearing her throat, Mari Nilsen's ex-husband is the new conductor for the Bergen Philharmonic. I was there for his debut concert last Thursday. And that's the reason I'm here, she repeats, and Vik shifts her legs, relieved that Nina's story might actually be leading somewhere.

*Bluebeard's Castle*, Nina says slowly and clearly. I don't know how familiar you are with—

Yes, Vik says, interrupting her, I'm familiar with it.

Well, precisely, Nina says, deflated. Safe to say it's a peculiar tale.

All of a sudden it hits her. Vik has read about her in *Bergens Tidende*, the arrogant professor who thinks that literary scholars would do a better job than the police when it comes to cracking cases like this one. The editorial team printed her words in bold letters with her name in black and white underneath them: 'We cannot entrust something as critical as police work to the police force!' She feels the blood pumping through her chest and throat and her cheeks flush red hot.

Well, no, it's not the most cheerful story, Vik says, clearly well aware of the plot and conclusion, signalling to Nina that this was a line of inquiry they've already checked out, naturally without being able to divulge any details of the investigation.

And as I'm sure you're already aware, Nina mumbles meekly, the choice of debut concert was intended as his nod to Mari Nilsen.

Gro Vik furrows her brow slightly, just sufficient to be noticeable.

That's according to Niklas Bull himself, Nina says, encouraged by the impression that this is news to Vik. In conversation with me.

A nod? Vik says.

Those were his words.

When was this?

Two days prior to the concert.

You two met?

I got in touch with him to find out her parents' names, she says, all fired up. She left a few things at the house—

What kind of things? Vik asks without hesitation.

Nothing really, Nina replies quickly. Just a box of old paperwork.

A box? Vik says, wearing an expression that confirms to Nina that it's both bewildering and entirely inexcusable for the previous owner not to bring such a discovery straight to the police.

Vik writes something down in her notebook while looking as if she's focusing hard on suppressing her irritation.

Was there anything else? she asks, looking up at Nina.

Nina hesitates. She doesn't want the meeting to end like this,

with a note to say that Nina neglected to bring potentially significant evidence to the police.

The opera, Nina says. It's all about, well, a Freudian take on
things would suggest that it's all about male rage at having been
betrayed.

Vik looks expectantly at Nina without making any further
notes.

And as I'm sure you're aware, Ask is not Niklas Bull's son.

Vik says nothing.

That was all, Nina says.

Thank you for that, Gro Vik replies curtly.

It's impossible to tell by looking at her whether Nina's contribution is utterly worthless, or whether it might, in fact, lead to a
breakthrough.

She feels a sudden wave of unease wash over her.

Obviously I'm not trying to suggest ... I've got no reason to
believe that Niklas Bull ... Nothing beyond what I've just told you,
she says, but Gro Vik shakes her head firmly.

We're grateful for any input. Was there anything else?

No, Nina says, and Vik switches off the recorder. She turns
away from Nina to face the screen and begins typing.

'The witness states that the conductor Niklas Bull, ex-husband
of the missing woman, dedicated an opera to her. The opera's
themes are murder and domestic violence.' Have I understood
things correctly?

Yes, Nina says. Or ... I mean, there are various interpretations.
The opera can also be said to depict our inner predator, or the act
of denying knowledge to others...

Gro Vik hesitates for a moment before returning to her key-
board.

'Murder, domestic violence, our inner predator or denying
knowledge to others,' she reads, and Nina nods. Gro Vik continues
typing.

'The witness also found a box belonging to the missing woman at Birkeveien 61, but handed this over to the woman's parents rather than to the police,' she reads.

Nina looks downcast as she acknowledges this addition.

Are you happy to confirm the accuracy of this statement?

I am.

Vik takes to her feet to indicate that the meeting is over, and Nina gets up, feeling as if she has been well and truly put in her place.

Call us if you think of anything else.

# Wednesday 12th December

In the wake of her humiliating meeting with the police, she trawls the internet for news about Mari Nilsen, for the last time, she tells herself. For once she's relieved not to discover anything new. She's neglected her master's students for the past few weeks, and her colleagues are still chasing her for a contribution to a project proposal on 'Representations of the self in the age of the algorithm'.

Two weeks of silence have passed. One witness reported a possible sighting on the coast-line bus to Bergen, but it remains unconfirmed. Before too long they'll announce that they're scaling back the search before Gro Vik eventually admits that they're making no progress, and the entire missing-persons case will be shelved.

Nina dutifully replies to that day's emails and is about to open the project proposal document when she receives a call from reception.

There's someone here to see you, a young man tells her.

Here? Nina says. Who?

Down at reception, the young man says. His name is—

Quick as a flash she desperately tries to recall some forgotten meeting or other, but she draws a blank.

She hears a brief exchange of words in the background before the man returns to speak to her.

Toralf Nilsen.

He's wearing a checked, woolly scarf, and holding a pair of soft, brown leather gloves in one hand, with the other clenched. Mari has her father's eyes, Nina thinks to herself as they sit down together in the university library café.

Sigrid doesn't know that I'm here talking to you, he says without preamble. He has a lilting Bergen dialect; he sounds gentle and quiet and far less full of the swagger of so many local men around his age.

I'd appreciate it if this conversation remained between us, he continues gravely.

Of course, Nina says.

I realised I'd need to speak to you alone, he says. Sigrid, she can be...

Nina forces herself not to offer suggestions as to how he might end that sentence, and Toralf Nilsen fails to elaborate.

How can I help you? she asks eventually.

He looks down at his hands, resting atop his gloves. He's still wearing his scarf. He closes his eyes, and she wonders if he might be in the early stages of dementia, suddenly finding that he's forgotten that he came to her, or even who she is.

The search is being scaled back, he finally tells her, and she feels her heart sink. He looks up and locks eyes with her.

Really? she says. Already?

They're getting nowhere.

She shakes her head slowly.

I read about you, he says. In the newspaper. Don't get me wrong, I know that you're not a private investigator...

Certainly not, she says.

But I think you make a good point, he continues. The police officers who've been to see us, it's as if they're asking all the wrong questions. They seem incapable of figuring out who Mari really *is*. They've got their own agenda, and Mari doesn't fit into it.

What do you mean by agenda? Nina asks, adding that she realises he doesn't mean it literally.

They think she wanted to disappear. And perhaps that's why there are so few leads. No mobile phone activity, no use of her bank cards. They're blinded by their bias.

What kind of bias?

The whole idea of the instable genius... he says, sounding resigned. The child prodigy who finds that she's unable to live up to the expectations of the outside world.

They think she's... Nina says, and he nods.

But that's not Mari. She's robust. A weary single mother, sure, but strong, full of life.

He shakes his head sadly.

Mari... he begins, ...she has this ability to *glow* like no one else.

And what do *you* think? she asks cautiously.

It's unthinkable. Mari would never leave Ask. Never. And we've tried telling them that.

He shakes his head again and repeats his words: Mari would never leave Ask.

There is such insistence in his expression that Nina nods wholeheartedly.

They don't know who Mari really *is*. That's the problem. But you... he says, looking up at her.

No, I— she begins, but he interrupts her.

They've given up on her, Toralf says, and a shadow of despair falls across his face.

Nina thinks back to the article in *Bergens Tidende* and blushes. To think she'd said all those things out loud.

Toralf Nilsen's chest rises and falls like that of an old, weary animal, he holds her gaze as he waits for her to break the silence.

Niklas Bull, she says, then falls silent.

What about Niklas?

You're still in touch?

I keep him up to date on things, he says. He's devastated.

And it hasn't occurred to you... she begins, and Toralf Nilsen looks up at her.

Might he ... have had anything to do with it?

He shakes his head firmly.

Never.

Nina falls silent, she doesn't mention Niklas Bull's debut concert, his grim nod to Mari.

Her decision to move to Bergen, she says eventually, unhurriedly. I can tell from your accent that you're from here yourself. Does Mari have family here?

No, he says. No one in Bergen.

So, moving out here, she says, after it ended between her and Niklas. What was the reasoning behind that?

He shrugs.

I mean, she had the house on Tornøy, didn't she? she says.

He looks down; silence envelops them.

Mari and Sigrid, he begins.

Her heart leaps, finally she'll find out what this is all about. She can still recall the awful feeling in her gut when she saw that Sigrid had seemingly received only one message from her daughter over the past few years, that was unless she made a habit of deleting them.

Toralf Nilsen rubs his hands on his thighs before looking up and pursing his lips as if whistling silently.

They weren't the best of friends, he began.

No, she says. Niklas said the same thing.

Most of their contact was through me, he says. But things had been better in the past year. Much better.

What's the reason for this ... frostiness? Sigrid has already told me about the argument they had on the day of her disappearance, when she heard that Mari had sold her instruments.

Yes, he nods. It ran deeper than that.

She says nothing, waiting for him to elaborate, keen not to interrupt him.

It started when Mari was pregnant, he says. He steals a glance at her. Niklas isn't... he says.

I know, she says, to what she reads as Toralf Nilsen's relief.

Sigrid, he begins, looking as if he's weighing up his words with great care. She's not the most effusive person. She's not that warm on the surface of things. When Mari fell pregnant, Sigrid couldn't see beyond the tens of thousands of hours of training she'd put in, all that hard work, her endless talent, all gone straight down the...

Toralf Nilsen pauses. Feeling tense, she waits for him to complete his sentence; he's not the type she'd expect to throw words like 'toilet' around in conversation.

Straight out the window, he says eventually. Mari was so insulted. Or rather, not insulted, that's not the word I'm looking for. *Hurt*, that's more like it. She'd expected to have our full support, and with good reason. She was going to be a single mother. But Sigrid, she wouldn't budge on the matter.

She cut contact?

Completely, he says, nodding.

And you...?

I tried talking sense into her, but it was all in vain.

But you and Mari, you kept in touch?

He falls silent, says nothing.

Things changed when Ask was born, he says quickly. Sigrid was enchanted with Ask once he'd arrived. She's a wonderful grandmother.

But? Nina says, trying to keep him on track.

But the argument that night caused everything to resurface. It all came flooding back to Mari. It was a reminder that her child hadn't ever been fully accepted. She wanted to take Ask back to Bergen that evening, but I managed to persuade her to stick around. I told her to go for a stroll, walk off her anger.

He falls silent once again.

The whole thing has left Sigrid paralysed, he says eventually. Paralysed by guilt, by fear.

But she doesn't think Mari's... she says, but holds back from completing her sentence. Because of one argument?

He looks down feebly.

At this moment in time, she doesn't know what to think about anything.

He seems so worn out, so weary and resigned that Nina feels the need to be pragmatic.

And she never mentioned who Ask's father was?

He looks up at her.

No.

But the police are looking into it?

Honestly, I couldn't tell you, Toralf says. They've asked us several times now, but none of us know anything about who he is.

You never spoke to Mari about it?

He says nothing.

It was a complete no-go?

Mari didn't want to talk about it, he says.

She doesn't have a close friend? Nina says. Someone she was able to open up to more than anyone else?

Sadly not, he says.

No? she says. There wasn't anyone she kept in touch with after moving to Bergen, or who she grew close to after that?

Mari's social life wasn't anything to write home about, he says. Music practice accounted for most of her time from an early age. Sigrid has spoken to her old friends on Tornøy, but none of them kept in touch with her. Or rather: Mari never replied when they *did* try getting in touch.

He gets up.

I don't want to take up any more of your time, he says. But we'd be incredibly grateful if you would consider helping us.

With what? Nina thinks, nodding in spite of herself.

Here's my mobile number, he says, passing her a slip of paper. Sigrid... he says, then falls silent. I think it's best if any communication stays between us, he says.

# Friday 14<sup>th</sup> December

They are shown into the office, where two leather chairs have been positioned opposite the desk.

She'll be right with you, the secretary says. Coffee or tea?

No thank you, Mads replies, both of them taking a seat.

Now then, have you missed me? he asks.

Us widows of the city council have our own survival strategies. I've not been lonely, in any case.

No?

Mari Nilsen's father came to see me at work the day before yesterday.

Really?

They've scaled back the search.

Already? Mads says, looking at her. He's sure?

Yes, it's early on, isn't it? But they were getting nowhere.

But surely they have a theory of some sort? Mads says.

According to her father, the police think she probably wanted to disappear. Since there are so few clues.

But?

Her parents refuse to believe it. And I understand why. They're supposed to sit there and accept the idea that their own daughter has chosen to abandon them, to abandon her own son?

Mads shakes his head without uttering a word.

I'm starting to wonder, Nina says.

Wonder about what?

All this about the baby's father. Mari didn't want to talk to anyone about it, it simply wasn't up for discussion. Could she have been the victim of an assault? Could Ask be the result of a...

He looks at her.

But surely she would have said something to her husband, rather than letting it all end in divorce? he suggests.

Could that be the reason she moved to Bergen? Nina continued, ruminating further. If Ask's father lives on Tornøy ... she'd have to get away from him.

Are you being serious?

Pfft, I don't know, she says. Let's talk about something else.

Mads pulls his iPad out of his bag.

Take a look at this, he says, turning the screen so she can see it.

'Modern quayside development', she reads, wrinkling her nose. Not you as well?

He shrugs.

You're quite literally on the waterfront, he says. Might be worth thinking about?

You really want to spend your twilight years surrounded by a pack of nouveau-riche psychopaths?

I think they're middle-aged millionaires, for the most part.

The door opens and their lawyer enters.

Now then, Berg says with a smile. Apologies for the wait.

She sits down at the desk and looks at them with a secretive smile.

I think I've got some good news for you both, she finally says. The council have accepted all of our demands, provided things are resolved swiftly. They want to take ownership as soon as possible.

How soon? Nina asks.

As soon as possible, their lawyer repeats. Around New Year, ideally.

New Year? Mads says. But that's less than three weeks away.

Berg nods. She slides a stack of paper in their direction.

I'll run you through everything point by point.

## Saturday 15th December

Forty flat-pack cardboard boxes stacked in four neat piles fill the living room. It's a start. An affluent couple in their sixties, she thinks to herself, thirty-five years under the same roof. How many boxes would be needed to accommodate their lives?

The contents of the kitchen cupboards alone will fill five, she says. And the wardrobe? Gosh, ten?

See this as a golden opportunity, Mads says. He is inside the wardrobe, knee-deep in coat hangers, stuffing clothing into bin bags.

Out with the old and in with the new.

I don't want the new, she says.

He tears off a bin bag and passes her the roll.

Start with anything you haven't worn in the last year.

And what about the plants? she asks, casting a despondent glance at the windowsill downstairs. What if we end up having to rent for months on end before we find somewhere?

Then we'll take our plants with us, he says. It'll all work itself out. Leave them for now.

She heads into the office, grabs a stack of newspapers from the desk and tears out sheet after sheet. She takes photographs down from the picture hooks on the wall, wrapping them in newspaper and stacking them up on top of one another on the desk. Then she leaves the room and goes downstairs, heading for the living room. She begins removing framed photographs from the walls.

A pale rectangle is revealed behind every picture. The walls are covered in marks left by whatever has been removed, wrapped in newspaper and neatly boxed up.

She stares at the picture of her grandparents, taken in the garden one summer in the 1930s, both wearing straw hats. Her grandmother is wearing a long, pale dress and clutching a bamboo badminton racket.

In the picture a little further along the wall, her parents have been photographed wearing the same hats thirty years later, with the same badminton rackets in the same spot in the garden.

Nina stands in the foreground, gap-toothed and grinning.

Taking a stroll down memory lane? Mads asks behind her.

I'm surprised, she says. I didn't think permanence mattered so much to me.

And yet?

She places the final photograph in the box.

I feel the same way the monarchy would if the public suddenly decided it was time to do away with them. Someone has come along out of nowhere and decided that I am to be removed, along with every moment of history that has gone before me.

And there was me thinking that you were a republican, Mads remarks.

Precisely. I was, she says, placing the lid on the box.

## Sunday 16<sup>th</sup> December

Oh my God, Ingeborg says, making straight for the windows. That view.

Ugh, no, Nina says, glancing quickly around her. Your father wouldn't like it here.

*You* wouldn't like it, you mean, Ingeborg says.

A large, blonde mane of hair emerges from one of the bedrooms and introduces herself, entirely unnecessarily, as the agent.

Yes, this place certainly lends itself to a desirable urban lifestyle, she says, facing Ingeborg. Exclusive shops and restaurants just a few floors down in the lift.

My mother's the one house-hunting, Ingeborg says, nodding briefly in Nina's direction.

I see, the agent says, looking somewhat flustered, suddenly required to think on her feet to present the advantages of the apartment with Nina in mind.

All on one level, she says. Very practical.

Isn't it? You're not going to be young forever, you know, Ingeborg remarks in agreement.

This is one of only three Premium Plus apartments, the agent says. That gives you a parking spot in the und—

We'll take a look around, Nina interrupts, making it clear that she'd much rather be left in peace.

Look at the appliances, all NEFF, Ingeborg says starry-eyed. Do you have any idea how much those cost?

A million kroner? Nina suggests, gazing critically at the extravagant advent-candle arrangement that the agent has placed in the middle of the dining table.

I'd kill for this kitchen.

That may be the case, but some of us have lower thresholds for committing murder. I take it you haven't considered doing a bit of extra training in the field of euthanasia?

On that subject, her daughter says, poking her head into the bathroom, how's it all going with the missing tenant?

Ingeborg, Nina whispers. It isn't a murder investigation.

Well, not yet, maybe, Ingeborg says. But a young mother walking out on her child just like that, and for what? A 'wonderful urban lifestyle'?

Most mothers imagine what it might be like to walk out on their impertinent children from time to time, Nina says, raising an eyebrow in Ingeborg's direction.

Ha ha, she says, very funny. But actually following through? Respect.

This might not be the most suitable topic of conversation for someone in your condition, Nina says, nodding at her daughter's stomach, which is just beginning to swell beneath her open coat.

Where's her son now, then?

With his grandparents. He's in good hands.

With his grandparents, Ingeborg repeats, her nose wrinkling slightly. Why not with his father?

Nobody knows who his father is, Nina says, and her daughter turns to look at her with interest.

They don't? But what about that guy in the newspaper, the ex-husband?

No, Nina says, shaking her head.

Ooh, polished concrete, Ingeborg whispers dreamily. She steps out of the bathroom and heads into the largest of the bedrooms, where the same smooth, sterile surfaces surround them.

I'm starting to understand why you like it so much here, Nina says. It's just like a hospital.

Ingeborg says nothing as she runs her fingertips along the perfectly smooth walls.

They could stick a gynaecology chair there, Nina says, nodding at the furthest corner of the room, and a little cabinet for blood samples just there.

Mum, Ingeborg says, turning around to face her. What are you actually looking for? *Soul*?

What's wrong with wanting a little soul! Nina says, throwing her arms out.

The agent's high heels ring out like tiny, piercing gunshots as she crosses the apartment.

Not bad, eh? she remarks with a foxy smile.

Ingeborg is just about to answer but is caught off guard by a yawn.

Well, do let me know if you have any questions, the agent says indignantly before turning and leaving the room.

Tired? Nina says.

It's Milja, Ingeborg says. She's been having nightmares lately.

Oh?

Witches and lions and frogs galore.

That's odd, Nina replies innocently. These are nice floors, in any case.

Dinesen flooring, her daughter tells her. Mum, this is a no-brainer.

Over my dead body, Nina says.

They're taking over the house in about two weeks.

I'm well aware of that, thank you, Nina says. But we'll rent somewhere until we find something that's right for us. We're not buying something on impulse. Anyway, the prospect of a coffee downstairs isn't entirely abhorrent to me, what do you say?

Together they make for the door without bidding the agent farewell. She glances up at them from where she stands, her telephone clamped between her ear and shoulder.

So, a secret lover, Ingeborg says once they've settled at a table by the window in the café on the ground floor. That's a bit racy.

What's that?

Your tenant. She's obviously had a secret lover here in the city, since she moved here from Tornøy, wasn't that what you told me? A married man who's bumped her off in a moment of panic.

It was a long-drawn-out moment of panic, in that case, Nina replies, her son is three years old.

Maybe it's only now, further down the line, that she's started nagging him to leave his family? Ingeborg suggests. She was a musician, wasn't she?

Yes.

It could be Leif Ove Andsnes, Ingeborg gasps.

You mean the pianist? Nina says. Thanks for the hot tip. I'll make sure to take that to the police.

Have you spoken to them?

I have actually, yes, Nina says, but I don't know how productive it was, to be honest.

They sip their coffee and look out onto the street. Christmas carols play in the background and the scent of rosemary, orange and cranberry fills the café.

Given that we did once pay for you to take piano lessons, Nina says, pulling her bag onto her lap, perhaps you might be able to make something of this?

She pulls out of her bag the old notebook she took from Mari Nilsen's box and passes it to Ingeborg.

What's this?

It's from the box you found in your cellar.

What are *you* doing with it?

Shh, Nina says, raising a hand to hush her. A bit of discretion, please. It fell out of the box, I'm going to take it back.

Ingeborg glances furtively around her before opening the notebook.

The strange thing is that Mari Nilsen had sold her violins and had supposedly turned her back on music by this point in time, Nina whispers.

Ingeborg leafs through the notebook.

You need to call them, she says.

Call who?

The police.

But why?

It's a diary.

Nina smiles indulgently.

Really? Read it, then, go on, she says. It's just an awful lot of musical jargon.

Mum, Ingeborg says with a resigned expression. It's a *diary*. This is all about her state of mind, it's got nothing to do with music.

And when exactly did you become an expert in people's frame of mind? Nina asks, but Ingeborg opens a page and lays the notebook out flat in front of her.

Twenty-fifth of September 2018, Birkeveien, Ingeborg reads. *Scherzoso*.

Nina gazes at her inquisitively.

Playful, Ingeborg says, resigned in the face of her mother's ignorance. She reads on.

First of October, Birkeveien. *Doloroso*.

Yes?

Melancholy! Ingeborg says. The following week: *Amoroso*. Surely you understand that one? Sixth of October: *Pesante*. Heavy. Two days later: *Con fuoco*.

Con...?

Fiery.

Nina furrows her brows and gazes at the pages with fresh eyes, the neat, cursive, old-fashioned handwriting.

Quite a range of emotions, Nina says. Fiery one day, heavy the next. Certainly something for a single mother with a part-time job and no doubt plenty of other things to keep her busy.

Ingeborg cocks her head to one side.

Well, she says, flicking through the notebook. Hardly surprising that she's a little up and down, given that it's all about her lover.

What did she write about her lover?! Nina asks, snatching the notebook.

My God, and *you* call yourself a professor of literature? Ingeborg says, grabbing the notebook straight back. You need to read between the lines.

She places a finger on the next entry: Here, take a look at this one for example, fifteenth of October, Birkeveien. *Allegro assai.* Ingeborg looks at Nina with an aloof expression. Lively. Hm? Next: *scherzoso.* Playful. Then: *amoroso.*

They could still just be referring to her frame of mind, Nina says.

*Con brio*, Ingeborg reads. With vigour.

Nina shrugs.

*Zitternd*, Ingeborg reads. Trembling.

It doesn't necessarily *have* to refer to a lover, Nina says.

*Come prima*, Ingeborg says. *Vivacissimo*!

Meaning?

Like the first time. Very lively!

Like the first time? Nina asks, inquisitive.

Ingeborg nods and turns the page.

*Sospirando*, sighing, *ziehen* and *zögernd,* it's dragging on, she's doubtful, expectant. *Lamentoso*, mournful.

Nina looks at her.

She's waiting for her lover to leave his wife for her, Ingeborg explains.

Nina cranes her neck to see for herself.

*Morendo*, Ingeborg reads quietly, laying the book down.

She looks at her mother.

Yes? Nina says.

Dying, Ingeborg says.

Is that what it means? Nina says, looking at Ingeborg. Dying?

Yes.

Let me see, Nina says, tugging the book from Ingeborg's hands. This is the very last entry, dated the fifteenth of November.

Dying? Nina asks. What's dying? Love? The relationship?

Mari herself? Ingeborg suggests. She wrote it just a few weeks before she disappeared, after some intense ups and downs in the relationship.

Judging by this, she must have been bipolar, at the very least, Nina says.

Hard to say whether it was her relationship or Mari herself that was bipolar, Ingeborg says slowly, taking the book once again and flicking back and forth through its pages.

Both, probably. This is classic psychopathic behaviour, Ingeborg says, blowing hot and cold from one day to the next, it's clear he's got her in an iron grip.

Let me see, Nina says impatiently.

She'll turn up before too long, Ingeborg says. But not alive.

# Tuesday 18<sup>th</sup> December

Kaia is on the telephone, sitting at her desk when Nina pokes her head in.

Wait a second, Kaia mouths, raising her palm.

Nina removes Kaia's coat from the chair opposite her and takes a seat.

Kaia very quickly scribbles something down on a pad of paper in front of her as she shakes her head. Eventually she says 'goodbye' and puts the phone down.

Idiots, she says.

Nina pulls the three Freud articles from her bag and slides them across the desk in Kaia's direction. She'd forgotten that she had them. Her bag had been hanging on a peg beneath her winter coat in her office. It had reappeared when the heating had turned itself off and she had started to feel the cold.

Kaia glances at the papers and then at Nina.

Yes? she says, pushing her glasses up on top of her head.

You're familiar with them? Nina says.

Am I familiar with *Freud*?

Are you familiar with these articles in particular? Nina says.

Kaia peers down at the papers once again, her lips moving ever so slightly as she flicks through the sheets of paper.

Well, it's not exactly little-known material, if that's what you're thinking, she says eventually.

No?

What are you doing with them, anyway? she asks, waving the sheets of paper at her.

It's an interdisciplinary project.

You're working on a project on *Übertragungsliebe*? she says, looking puzzled.

On what now?

Kaia looks at her, surprised.

Transference love?

Transference love? Nina repeats.

Surely you're familiar with transference! Kaia retorts indignantly. So much for being a seasoned academic!

I've had quite enough of people calling my academic integrity into question lately, Nina says.

Literary studies is the one remaining comfort us poor, unfortunate psychoanalysts have left; it'll soon be the only field that continues to acknowledge Freud's work.

Of course, Nina says, offended, obviously I'm aware of his work, but it's hardly something I come across on a daily basis. Feel free to refresh my memory.

Kaia clasps her hands behind her head and leans back in her office chair.

Well, put very simply, transference refers to the feelings that a patient develops for the person treating them. It needn't necessarily be romantic love, but in many cases that's exactly the form it takes.

Transference love, Nina says, and Kaia nods.

Way back in the early days of psychoanalysis, Freud couldn't help but notice that all of the young women suffering with hysteria and undergoing therapy fell head over heels in love with their therapists. I'm sure you're familiar with Anna O., for example? She experienced a phantom pregnancy because she was convinced she'd conceived a child with Freud's colleague, Joseph Breuer. Breuer panicked and fled that evening, off on honeymoon with his wife, no less, Kaia says with a chortle.

Charming.

Or Ferenczi, Kaia continued, who treated both his lover *and* her daughter, Elma, who he later fell in love with and wanted to marry.

What a mess, Nina says, rolling her eyes.

No doubt about that. Psychoanalysis as a field of thought was running itself into the ground even in its infancy; therapists and patients crossed every possible barrier over and over again.

Kaia gets up and looks at the bookshelf while continuing to speak.

Freud wasn't so stupid that he thought patients falling for their therapists left, right and centre was mere coincidence; and therapists couldn't possibly allow themselves to believe that they were as desirable as their patients would have them think. On the contrary, it was the therapeutic situation that released these overwhelming emotions. According to Freud, it is virtually inevitable that a patient should fall in love with their therapist.

Goodness me, Nina says, listening to Kaia's explanation with growing interest. It was *these* particular articles that Mari Nilsen wanted to translate. That can't be a coincidence, can it?

That might be overstating things, Kaia continues, but even today, erotic feelings or passionate relationships between a patient and his or her therapist are widespread. Because in addition to transference love, you also have *counter*transference love, she says, which are the feelings that the therapist has for their patients – male therapists account for the majority of cases, but female therapists are susceptible to the phenomenon, too. And just to illustrate how interwoven these feelings are with the therapeutic setting: even *I've* had a host of patients fall for me, men in their twenties declaring that they can't stop thinking about me!

How flattering! Nina says, clapping her hands.

Certainly, at least for those who manage to convince themselves that the feelings their patients are having are specific to *them*. But I'm not that daft. It's a punishable offence, Kaia says, taking advantage of patients' dependency and vulnerability like that. Above all, it strongly suggests the existence of an unresolved case of narcissism on the part of the therapist, so they deserve everything they get, she says, pulling a thick volume from a shelf and slapping it down on the desk in front of Nina.

But Freud managed to turn all this to the advantage of psycho-analysis, she says proudly. He viewed transference as a *tool*, rather than a problem in itself. It could offer valuable insight into the patient's condition and could prove beneficial to their treatment if, and only *if*, the therapist was capable of maintaining a certain professional distance and controlling their own potential counter-transference.

And it's called transference because…?

Because an individual transfers his or her feelings, desires or attitudes towards their parents or other important figures from their childhoods onto their therapists. That was Freud's theory, at least. People see things a little differently today, Kaia says.

Nina leaps up all of a sudden. She needs to find out if Mari Nilsen was seeing a psychologist. Given the shift in temperament expressed in her diaries, it's clear she experienced major fluctuations in her mood, but who'd know about that? Niklas Bull, if she was undergoing treatment while they were still married. Her parents, perhaps.

Are you off? Kaia asks, surprised.

Nina imagines Mari Nilsen fleeing the country with her married psychologist, leaving everything behind – perhaps even Ask? Is it really possible that some sort of wild, romantic, intoxicated infatuation with her psychoanalyst might have brought her to the point of abandoning everything? Or worse, that she might have fled *from* him? Or worse still—

Hello? Kaia says. Is anybody home?

She peers over her spectacles at Nina with a resigned expression.

I have to go, Nina says, disappearing out the door.

Are we still having fish soup at yours before the concert this evening? Kaia calls after her.

She stands there, phone in hand, doing her best to control her breathing.

First a Bartók opera, now Sigmund Freud. If Gro Vik wasn't already convinced that Nina was a ridiculous fool, she'd certainly think so now.

Bartók, Freud and a few musical annotations in Italian and German. It sounds so completely far-fetched when she runs through how she might explain it to the detective inspector.

She hangs up. Better to take it directly to Niklas Bull and Mari's parents. She grabs her coat from the hook, picks up her bag and leaves the office, hurrying down the various flights of stairs and out into the dark December afternoon. The light that radiates from the Christmassy streets of the central district envelops the whole city like a blanket; she walks at a quick pace, the tarmac wet underfoot, shoving past the oversized bags of the students who crowd the narrow pavement on her way to Grieg Hall.

She's given a message to let her know that Niklas Bull will be with her as soon as they've finished their run-through of the *Christmas Oratorio*.

She takes a seat at a table in the foyer and pulls up Toralf Nilsen's number.

He picks up straight away with hope in his voice; they're tip-toeing around, waiting for a phone call to tell them that Mari has been found, preferably safe and well.

It's just me, Nina, she says. Wisløff. Nothing to report, unfortunately.

The pause that follows is steeped in disappointment.

Are you out walking? she asks eventually. I can't hear you very well.

It's the wind, he says. We're down by the water with Ask. Wait a second, I'll find a sheltered spot.

*Don't go out any further, Ask!* she hears Sigrid shout in the background.

The roar of the blustering gale disappears and he sounds closer, clearer.

Is this any better?

I don't have anything to report, as I say, Nina says apologetically, just a question for you. Do you happen to know if Mari is seeing or has ever seen a psychologist?

A psychologist, Toralf repeats slowly, as if the word is unfamiliar to him. No, that's—

A psychologist or psychiatrist or any form of therapist? No?

No, Toralf replies with a sigh. No, I can't say I know about anything along those lines.

And what about Sigrid, might she know anything?

She hears him move the phone away from his face, and the

crackling in the microphone starts up again. He disappears for a moment before the wind falls silent and his voice returns.

No, he says. We don't know anything about that.

Oh well, she says. That's fine.

But she's very interested in all that, he says. She reads books on psychology. She reads books on all sorts of topics, always has.

She reads books on psychology, Nina repeats, disappointed. Perhaps it's as simple as all that, she thinks to herself. Just an interest.

Well, Nina says, thank you for that.

Ask is launching his boat, Toralf says, I'm afraid I have to go.

He comes downstairs with a cup of coffee in one hand, his curls in disarray. She stands up and waves and he catches sight of her.

Thanks for making the time to see me, she says, as he pulls out a chair. I'll be brief.

Thank you, he says, there's a fair bit for us to get through before this evening's performance.

We're coming along, Nina says, my husband and I, and another couple. She immediately regrets saying so, she's making it sound as if her engagement is propping up the city's entire cultural sector, but Niklas Bull squeezes out a grateful smile.

What can I do to help? he asks, vaguely impatient.

Deciding to get straight to the heart of the matter, Nina asks: Can you recall if Mari has ever seen a psychologist?

A psychologist? Mari? he says, furrowing his brow and staring long and hard at Nina. No.

Her heart sinks.

You're quite sure?

She concealed it well if she did, he says.

Perhaps she did? Nina suggests. You were away an awful lot, touring during the time you two spent living on Tornøy, isn't that so? How can you be so sure?

He shakes his head.

I'd have known, he repeats with absolute certainty.

Who can Ask's father possibly be, then?! Nina says, resigned, and Niklas gazes at her, perplexed.

Is *that* what you think? he asks after a moment. That Mari had a child with her *psychologist*?

I *do* know that she was very interested in... Nina begins, but stops herself, it sounds silly when she says it out loud.

But if Mari wasn't seeing a psychologist, she says instead, might there be someone else she saw or spoke to or received some form of treatment from? Anything at all along those lines?

Niklas Bull stops fiddling with his *snus* tin. He hesitates. Pulls a used pouch of *snus* from under his top lip and slips it into the lid of the box.

Only during that winter she was ill, he says quietly.

Ill? she says, vaguely recalling him mentioning something about her being unwell during a previous conversation.

She had cancer, he says, slipping a new pouch of *snus* under his top lip.

Cancer? Nina says with surprise. Mari? When was that?

It wasn't that serious, he says quickly. It was all OK in the end.

When was this?

He closes his eyes, thinking back.

It must have been four years ago now, during the winter.

Really? Nina says, dumbfounded.

It was all over and done with in no time at all, he says in an attempt to moderate her excitement. She had surgery, then radio-therapy. It all went smoothly. Mari was strong, she was at peace with the whole thing.

Was? Nina says.

*At the time*, he emphasises with a certain degree of irritation, locking eyes with her. I don't think she's dead, if that's what you're insinuating.

So where did she undergo treatment? Nina asks.

Haukeland University Hospital.

Haukeland, she repeats. Winter four years ago. And you don't think she might have been seeing a psychologist in connection with that?

No, he says.

No, well, I'm sure you'd know, Nina says. You were there, after all.

He says nothing.

Or...? she begins, with barely concealed loathing.

Yes, he says, nodding.

Nina sees him swallow.

I was busy with work at the time.

I see.

I was in London for a period, he says, looking down. The BBC Concert Orchestra. It was an unmissable opportunity.

It sounds it, Nina says. London. While Mari was being treated for cancer here in Bergen.

Well, when you put it like that... he objects. But it was Mari who insisted. She didn't want to hold me back.

Of course. It was an unmissable opportunity, she says, quoting his own words back at him.

Niklas Bull has turned pale.

I'm not here to judge, she says in an effort to placate him. I'm sure it was very difficult for you too.

He says nothing.

And Mari was strong, as you say.

He is silent, fiddling with his *snus* tin.

Surgery followed by radiotherapy, she says.

It was an error of judgement, he says, so quietly that she can barely hear him, and she nods.

He bows his head, his throat crimson.

But the times you *were* present, she says, attempting to be pragmatic. Did you ever meet her doctor? Do you happen to recall a name?

He shakes his head.

Was it a woman? A man?

I don't know.

You don't know?

He says nothing.

You were never there?

I was working, he mumbles.

What type of cancer was it? she asks, exasperated.

He seems to hesitate.

Something to do with the salivary glands, he says eventually, looking up at her almost inquisitively.

Salivary gland cancer? she asks, sceptical.

It's rare, he says.

And Ask was born in…? she asks.

He thinks for a moment.

November, wasn't it? Her due date?

I don't know.

November, December, January … February, or thereabouts, she says. Where was she at that point in time?

As I say, I was in London, he says. And Mari was undergoing treatment.

A ringtone breaks the silence. He picks up his phone, checks the screen, looks up at her.

I'm going to have to…

She nods, and he turns around and leaves, his telephone pressed to his ear.

When she gets home, Mads is standing in the kitchen with a leek in one hand and a knife in the other. He casts a curious glance in her direction.

Oh my God, she says.

You forgot? he says.

I forgot.

Well, he says, fish soup without fish it is.

I can run to the supermarket down the road, Nina says guiltily.

He glances up at the wall clock.

I've spent all day on my backside, I could do with the walk.

Anything I can do in the meantime?

You could always set the table, he says.

As soon as he's out of the door, she pulls her laptop from her briefcase and sits at the kitchen table. 'Transference doctor', she types in the search box, and is immediately faced with an enormous number of returns on her search, but closer inspection reveals that most are concerned with psychologists and their patients.

She is just about to close the lid of her laptop when she catches sight of a hit from the Norwegian Medical Association's online journal. She opens the article, which reveals itself to be an explicit investigation of transference in doctor-patient relationships.

As she continues to read, her pulse beginning to race, she hears the front door open and instinctively closes the lid of the laptop, in spite of the fact that she has nothing to hide, strictly speaking.

From the porch she hears Kaia's familiar tones.

Come on up, Nina shouts.

Kaia soon appears at the top of the stairs, her cheeks and the tip of her nose rosy red after walking through the city in the cold snap.

Are you *working*? she asks in disbelief. Where's Mads?

Off out to get some fish, Nina replies, anyway, never mind Mads: where's Jo?

He's going to meet us at Grieg Hall, he had to work.

Kaia looks around her.

Redecorating? she says teasingly, nodding at the various cardboard boxes stacked up against the walls and the pale rectangles on the walls where photographs and paintings and prints once hung.

Oh, ha ha, Nina says, before flashing her an accusatory look. Thanks so much for your misleading lecture, by the way.

What are you talking about? Kaia asks, pulling out a chair. She unravels her scarf from around her neck and wraps it around her hands to warm them through as she gazes at her sister-in-law quizzically.

Transference! It's everywhere! Look at this, Nina says, opening the laptop and turning it around so Kaia can see the screen.

Hey, hey, Kaia says, attempting to appease Nina with the wave of a hand. Calm down. She quickly scans the screen and shrugs.

Ask a psychoanalyst and you'll get a psychoanalyst's take on things. You have *our* transference, and then you have a more general, watered-down version, she says, rising above the criticism levelled in her direction.

Well, the general, watered-down version makes much more sense in my mind, Nina says. The idea that transference exists in all sorts of human relationships, that it doesn't necessarily have all that much to do with one's relationship with one's parents.

Was there supposed to be white wine to go with this soup I was promised? Kaia asks, getting up and opening the fridge. Surely you haven't packed all of your glasses just yet?

Are you mad? Nina remarks dryly.

It's not our fault that ordinary folks have nabbed our phenomenon and applied it to any old situation, Kaia continues, twisting the corkscrew with ease.

But when people start to believe that they've fallen in love with prominent politicians or managers or coaches, Nina says, then in reality it could simply be a case of transference? A psychological process – passing madness, in other words?

Hmm, Kaia says, taking a sip of her wine. Falling in love is a kind of madness in its own right. I'm not sure what would constitute falling in love and what would be considered transference. Perhaps falling in love is simply one of various examples of transference. But what *is* certain is that transference is highly likely to occur in any kind of relationship that extends over a period of time and that features some imbalance of power. It could be a teacher and their student, perhaps even their school pupil, or a manager and their employee. Or a doctor and a nurse, for that matter.

Or a doctor and patient?

Certainly. You need an imbalance of power and an individual who needs someone to admire. Possibly even someone who needs to *be* admired. Various things can occur if those conditions are met. If the teacher or coach or doctor isn't aware of this process, he is at risk of responding to transference love, and in certain circumstances, that's a serious offence. Like at the university, for instance, didn't they make changes to forbid relationships between students and teaching staff a few years ago?

That was nothing to do with me, Nina says. I've never had my way with any of my students.

What sort of project *is* this, exactly?

Psychoanalytical literary theory, Nina says breezily. It's nothing new. The narrative desires of the reader and so on.

Kaia flashes her a sceptical look.

*Fine.* You know, Mari Nilsen...

Your missing tenant? Kaia asks.

That's the one, Nina says. Well today I found out that she was being treated for cancer here in the city for a short while. And she was very interested in transference...

I see, Kaia says.

You do?

It's a textbook example, Kaia says. You fear for your life, and then he or she pops up out of nowhere: a demigod in a white coat, there to save you. You'd hardly be human if you didn't develop feelings of some sort for this guardian angel. And that's perfectly OK, as long as the doctor doesn't take advantage of the patient's adoration.

But Mari, Nina says. She fell pregnant.

With her doctor's baby? Kaia asks, dumbfounded.

It's one theory.

Well, well, well, Kaia says, one eyebrow raised. That'd be someone's medical licence out the window, in any case. But do you think this might have something to do with her disappearance?

I'm not sure, Nina says.

I thought it was this Bluebeard conductor chap who was the prime suspect?

Nina shrugs.

The strange thing about transference, Kaia says, taking a sip of her wine, is that the more distant and impersonal the doctor, the more powerful the feelings of love that develop on the part of the patient.

Really?

Doctors probably think that keeping their distance will ensure that they'll have a more straightforward relationship with their patients, but the irony is that such distance provides the patient with greater scope to develop illusions about the doctor.

So doctors can't do wrong for doing right, essentially?

Well, Kaia says, it's not exactly impossible to navigate such a landscape. Everything goes smoothly in the majority of cases.

So the patient has to ask themselves: would I love this man in the same way if he happened to be a plumber I met at the supermarket? Nina says.

Or vice versa: if a pipe in my cellar sprang a leak, would I love this plumber in the same way as I would if he happened to be a doctor I met at the supermarket? Kaia says. The context has as much a part to play as the person. Either way, the responsibility lies with the person in the position of power. It's part of the contract: the patient or the student, or whoever it is, can't help the fact that transference love occurs. It's almost their ordained *role* to attempt to seduce their doctor, coach, mentor, whoever! And it's the doctor or coach or mentor's duty and responsibility *not* to respond to these feelings.

So those who do respond, Nina says, what's the deal there?

The door opens downstairs. The familiar sound of Mads hanging up his coat and slotting his shoes into place on the shoe rack.

He makes his way upstairs, triumphantly wielding a bag.

Fresh haddock!

Those who've studied it at length have discovered certain commonalities. A number have clear narcissistic traits, Kaia says, with a nod in Mads' direction.

What's that? Mads asks, beginning to unwrap the fish.

Oh nothing, Nina says, winking at Kaia.

They've typically achieved a position of leadership as far as their careers are concerned, and they've started to believe that ordinary ethical standards no longer apply to them. It's good, old-fashioned, unscrupulous exploitation of their position. They tend to claim that it does no harm to the patients, and it does tend to be patients, *plural*. They claim quite the contrary, in fact.

And is there anything in that? Nina says.

Well, it's hard to say, Kaia replies. Different people react to abuse in very different ways. We're talking about a relationship of trust, a symbiotic bond. When that kind of trust is exploited, the consequences can be significant.

Obviously.

But the majority of therapists who've embarked upon a relationship with a patient – and it does tend to be a middle-aged man and a young female patient, though the same goes for female therapists – claim that they're genuinely in love with the patient, and justify the relationship on those terms. They claim that they're soulmates, that they'd be married if only they'd met under different circumstances, Kaia says.

Oh, of course! Nina replies.

And they often have a need to be idolised or loved by their patients, to feed their own self-esteem, Kaia says, grasping her glass.

Have you ever experienced this, Mads? Nina asks.

Experienced what? he replies, craning his neck out of the kitchen, away from the overpowering aromas.

A patient falling in love with you.

My God, Mads says. If I had a krone for every time that had happened, you'd be married to a wealthy man.

Hilarious.

It's true, Mads says, turning to face them. If only you knew, you'd realise that being married to a senior consultant is a risky business. You two have no idea, he says gravely. And as for a city council, well! All those political advisors and anonymous case workers, the world and his wife craving my appreciation...

Well, here's to you, Nina says, topping up her glass.

Any chance of a tipple for the chef? Mads asks, taking a glass from the cupboard.

I found out something interesting today, Nina tells Mads. Mari Nilsen was treated for cancer at Haukeland University Hospital.

Really? Mads says.

At the same time she fell pregnant, she says, drawing breath.

It was only a few days ago that you were talking about sexual assault on Tornøy, but now it's her doctor in the frame?

I'm not joking, Nina says. It's strange that she should become so fascinated by transference in the aftermath, so much so that she even tried to publish a book on the subject.

Yes, Kaia says, that *is* odd.

Mads busies himself chopping carrot and celeriac.

Peculiar, he says.

What is?

It was one of Jo's colleagues who tipped me off about her. That she needed somewhere to stay. A doctor.

Are you sure? Nina asks him, wide-eyed. Do you know who?

No, he says, but Jo will.

It'll be that Me Too doctor, I'm telling you now, Kaia says.

Huh? Nina says.

That senior consultant in Jo's department who there were all those warnings about, Kaia says.

Could well be, Mads says, but I doubt they were responsible for impregnating her.

What do you know about it? Nina says.

Well, that consultant is a woman, for one thing.

Modern technology's come a long way, but not quite *that* far, Kaia remarks dryly.

Jo is standing with a glass in his hand, chatting to a younger couple just inside the foyer as they make their way up the steps leading into Grieg Hall, surrounded by the flicker of torches, frosty mist and floor-length wool coats. He turns away from the pair and approaches them as they enter, taking Kaia and Nina's coats as he balances his glass first in one hand, then the other. He and Mads go to hang up the group's coats before heading to the bar, while Kaia and Nina stand in the middle of the foyer, nodding at acquaintances.

I forgot to ask about the house hunt, Kaia says. Anything new on that front?

Nina shakes her head in frustration as Kaia rolls her eyes.

If only you could see how liberally I've expanded my search criteria! We'll be viewing places out in Loddefjord any day now, at this rate!

I imagine that would probably be the first time you'd ever set foot there, eh? Kaia says.

Mads and Jo return, both carrying a glass of wine in each hand.

Jo passes them their glasses. May I join you ladies, he says, into one big lady?

Mads gives a brief chuckle while Kaia stares blankly at him.

Groucho Marx? Jo says. No, nothing?

What are your plans for Christmas? Kaia asks, turning to Nina.

Packing what's left of our lives into a few cardboard boxes and driving them out to a cold and soulless storage unit, I imagine, Nina replies.

We're staying at home, Mads confirms. Ingeborg is with Eirik's parents this year.

Why not come over to ours for Christmas Eve, then? Kaia says, looking at Jo, who nods at her suggestion.

That might be nice, Nina says. Better than sitting alone in an empty house primed for demolition, I should think.

Mads nods and sips his wine.

Jo, Nina says, lowering her voice and resting a hand lightly on his back. Can you remember which of your colleagues tipped Mads off about renting the house to Mari Bull?

Gosh. I'll need to think about that. Why do you ask? he replies, gripping his concert programme.

At that moment the bell rings, and the crowd immediately begins filtering into the concert hall.

We can talk about it after, she says with the wave of a hand.

They set down their glasses and join the masses on their way inside.

Kielland, Jo says. That was it. She's doesn't work there anymore.

It was a woman? Nina says, deflated, and Jo nods.

You don't recall her first name?

Anne, maybe?

They find their row and shuffle past knees and hips and well-fed stomachs until they make it to their seats.

It was Mads who had bought the tickets, the most particular among them about where to sit; it should be central, but not *too* central, and close to the stage, but not *too* close.

Nina and Kaia sit down, a husband on each side of them. The musicians tune their instruments as the chorus waits behind them, quiet as church mice.

Just like last time, the hum of the audience in the concert hall falls silent in the space of just a few short seconds. Absolute silence grips the vast, dark space, they hear the clack of footsteps before they can make anything out. Then five people enter from the right, four soloists and the conductor in the middle, and applause breaks out.

Nina sits motionless without clapping. Kaia glances at her inquisitively.

Nina nods in the direction of the stage.

The five people on stage give deep bows. The conductor turns away and steps onto his podium.

What?

That's not Niklas Bull, she whispers to Kaia.

What?

*That's not Niklas Bull*, she repeats.

Perhaps he was never going to conduct this performance, Kaia whispers back before Jo raises a hand to hush them.

He was. I spoke to him earlier today.

How strange, Kaia manages to reply before the timpani interrupts her, followed by flutes and clarinets and violins and trumpets.

The thunderous opening leaves her whole body aquiver. Where is Niklas Bull? She glances down at the concert programme. His face adorns the cover.

She clasps her hands together and gazes nervously at the stage, trying to concentrate on the music but finding her focus quickly fading.

The conductor is a slim, older man, animated and brimming with enthusiasm. She tries to focus her attention on the orchestra and the chorus, but finds herself recalling every detail of the conversation she'd had with Niklas Bull earlier that day, he *had* mentioned that he'd be conducting the *Christmas Oratorio*, hadn't he? Surely?

It's always the same: the *Christmas Oratorio* begins well, but swiftly descends into a mishmash of recitatives and long-winded arias; in truth there are only a few highlights, all of which are now long past.

Nina peers at Mads. He's nodded off. He does the same thing every year. She lets him sleep; she can always give him a nudge if he starts snoring.

The deafening tones of the chorus stream in their direction, she feels hot, her legs are in the process of going to sleep. She shuffles in her seat. Kaia nudges her gently and nods at Jo – he, too, has drifted off.

She tries to turn her attention back to the chorus and the orchestra, but it is as if the chorus and the string musicians have come together to create a chaotic clamour. She squeezes her eyes closed, clears her throat and concentrates on her breathing as she listens intently. The chorus sounds more and more like the shrieking cacophony of a madhouse.

It hits her all of a sudden, a resounding gut punch.

Gro Vik.

All of this stuff about transference, doctors and patients, it's a dead end.

Gro Vik, she had followed up on what Nina had presented to her.

The breathless trumpets, the violins, they pierce her ears, cutting deeper and deeper, the thundering timpani causes her eardrums to quiver.

She had been right.

Bluebeard. Male rage at having been betrayed.

She leans in towards Kaia, her lips to her ears, warm skin and the scent of perfume.

He's been arrested.

Kaia turns to look at her, wide-eyed.

*It was Niklas Bull all along.*

The hall erupts into applause and the stamping of feet as the final trumpet falls silent. The unknown conductor bows deeply, fit to burst with pride, and all around Nina people take to their feet, the entire row in front of them, then Kaia jumps up, Mads and Jo too, their hands loudly pounding together.

Nina stands up slowly, gripping onto Mads, worried that her legs might not carry her.

# Wednesday 19ᵗʰ December

She sleeps badly that night. As soon as Mads steps out of the door the following morning, she rings Toralf, but there's no answer. She tries twice more to no avail. Eventually she pulls herself together in a hurry, finds the three cardboard boxes of things that need taking to Oldervik and carries them out to the car.

She makes it to the ferry at Halhjem for ten o'clock and drives straight on board.

She goes through her usual routine of checking the news on her phone during the crossing, attempting to find out if the arrest has been reported, but it's still early to make that sort of thing public. She sends Toralf a message to let him know that she's on her way before buying herself a cheese sandwich and a cup of coffee served in a flimsy paper cup. Garish paper chains have been hung randomly around the shop.

By the time the ferry is preparing to dock, she still hasn't heard back from Toralf. Could it be that he's being interviewed as a witness?

She files out along with the rest of the passengers, making her way down the steep stairs leading to the car deck. What was it that she had actually found out? As she climbs into her car, she wonders if she ought to leave the queue of traffic and join the cars on the other side waiting to go the opposite way, making her way straight back home instead.

The shutter ahead of them opens and the cars around her start up their engines. She slowly follows the car in front of her, emerging beneath the open sky.

On this side of the fjord, light snow billows in the air around them; she looks for a layby to indicate and turn the car into, but the queue of vehicles refuses to break up, a Nissan lingering on her tail like a horsefly, and she inches closer and closer to Oldervik until eventually it'd be too stupid to turn around and go home.

She pulls up in the front yard, carries the boxes inside, makes herself a cup of coffee then wanders restlessly around the cold house, waiting for a reply.

When the clock strikes one, she pulls on her coat and steps outside. Slowly she makes her way along the gravel path, gradually approaching the housing estate.

It's not ideal, turning up out of the blue like this yet again, but she's anxious to hear what's happened to Niklas Bull. To find out if things have progressed as she suspects they have.

The lawn is coated with frost. The thick layers of leaves covering the flower beds are frozen stiff. The clusters of heather in their various shiny pots on the front steps have all turned brown.

A large star hangs in the window, shining bright.

Toralf opens the door to her. He looks at her with surprise before moving to one side and inviting her in. She steps over the threshold and removes her shoes, Toralf takes her coat.

I'm sorry to be showing up at such short notice like this, Nina says, but he shakes his head. She's in the living room, he says.

It's eerily quiet in the house. Perhaps Ask is sleeping, she thinks to herself, even though it's late in the day for that. She climbs the stairs, taking each one slowly; the atmosphere beneath the bright, high ceiling has a strange edge to it. Nina spots her sitting on the sofa with her back to the door as she makes her way up the final few stairs.

Nina stands there for a moment, waiting.

Sigrid turns halfway, her face expressionless.

Is that you? she asks, her voice hollow.

Nina takes a step in her direction.

What's happened? she asks, almost without making a sound.

I thought you knew, Toralf says on the stairs behind her.

She turns around.

We found her yesterday, he says calmly.

He climbs the final few stairs himself and slowly makes his way across the room and over towards Sigrid. He places a hand on her shoulder before sitting beside her.

Nina stands there, unsure what to do with herself.

Come and sit down, Toralf says. The priest won't be here until two.

Slowly she crosses the room and sits directly opposite Sigrid without saying a word. She wants to hug her, but Sigrid is sitting motionless on the sofa, showing no hint of an invitation.

You didn't know? Toralf says.

I didn't, she whispers.

Sigrid makes no eye contact. Her grey hair hangs loose down to her shoulders, she's wearing a lightweight, moss-green, wool jumper and a pair of grey trousers. The wood burner is ablaze yet she appears cold, her shoulders pointing sharply upwards.

I thought it had already been in the papers, he says. It'll be out before long, I'm sure.

What...? she asks.

He lowers his gaze.

Where? she asks quietly.

Down here, Toralf says, his gaze fixed directly ahead of him. She was washed ashore by the water's edge. We were down there with Ask, as you know.

Just here? Nina whispers, she turns white, grips the arm of the sofa.

Sigrid looks down, raising her eyebrows slightly.

Toralf pats her knee gently.

There's nothing to indicate anything criminal, he says.

Sigrid shakes her head gently, her eyes lowered, the corners of her mouth drawn upwards to form an unnerving smile.

Are you sure? Nina asks. Has she been examined by the forensic...

No trace of anything in her blood, no external injuries, nothing, Toralf says.

Nothing besides what you'd expect to see after spending that long underwater, Sigrid adds dryly, a strange tone to her voice. Nina avoids making eye contact.

Nothing? So, it was an accident?

Toralf gives a light shrug.

We'll never know.

A strange place to fall, Sigrid replies with the same sickening half-smile.

They say that a person usually floats to the surface... Toralf begins, but his voice breaks, he clears his throat.

A person usually floats to the surface not far from where they drowned, Sigrid says, completing her husband's train of thought.

Nina falls silent.

Toralf stands up and makes his way into the kitchen. He returns with three mugs and a pot of freshly brewed coffee.

I'm afraid we haven't got anything else to offer you, he says, filling the mugs.

God, no, don't apologise, Nina says, I don't need anything.

They sit in silence. Steam rises from the mugs, which remain untouched.

But it doesn't make sense. Why would she... Nina begins, trailing off mid-sentence. When she had a son, she says eventually.

Toralf shakes his head.

None of us had any idea it was as bad as all this.

What do you mean?

You were the one who asked us if she'd been to see a psychologist, Sigrid interrupts bitterly, her tone filled with self-reproach.

That wasn't why... Nina begins, but stops herself.

It's obvious, Sigrid says, we have our answer. Chronic depression.

It's often those on the outside who are able to see things most clearly, Toralf says.

They're behaving so uncomfortably – eerily normally, under the circumstances, Nina thinks to herself. Here they are, sitting and chatting, making coffee and seeing visitors, as if nothing has changed.

We've had time to get used to the idea, Toralf says, as if he can read her mind. That she might not be coming home.

You're in shock, Sigrid tells her husband sharply. You're suppressing it.

Perhaps that's true, Toralf replies, no desire to start an argument.

They hear a sound at the front door, Ask's cheerful, chattering voice and someone with deeper, darker tones. The child clambers upstairs at full speed, bounding across the room in his grandparents' direction, but stopping in his tracks when he catches sight of Nina.

Hi there, Nina says, then jumps: Niklas Bull's dark curls appear at the top of the stairs. He seems equally surprised to see Nina.

It's you, he says, and she has to bite her tongue to prevent herself from expressing her surprise at the fact he hasn't been arrested after all.

He slept for three quarters of an hour or so, Niklas tells Sigrid.

Thank you, she replies flatly.

I'd forgotten how nice it is to walk around here, he says.

Niklas dropped everything to come here as soon as we... Toralf explains.

It's better to face grief together, Niklas says. And good to be able to help out.

He makes his way across the room and sits in the armchair with his legs crossed, pulling Ask up onto his lap and opening a book.

Nina looks at them; of everything she is feeling, grief is far from the top of the list. Hardly surprising – after all, she never knew Mari Nilsen. But what she does feel is disappointment. Disappointment that it's all over. Mari has been found, in the worst possible circumstances, and by those closest to her, most likely having taken her own life, there's no more to be done.

This is where it ends. Her ridiculous investigation.

A navy-blue estate car drives up the street, closer and closer until it pulls up outside.

That'll be the priest, Toralf says.

Nina gets up.

She doesn't know what to say. Toralf looks at her, downcast but grateful; Sigrid avoids eye contact. She stands there for a moment before turning around and making her way downstairs in silence.

Niklas approaches as she pulls on her coat by the front door. As he crosses the tiled floor, she can't tell if he intends to embrace her or reproach her.

You went to the police, he says, his voice low.

She looks up at him, there's no point in denying it.

Yes, she replies.

Why?

I thought I had information worth sharing.

They took me in for questioning again, he says. I sat there for hours, had to go over the most intimate details, jealousy, betrayal, they treated me like some sort of...

He stops, no anger in his eyes, only sadness.

I'm sorry, she says.

Amidst everything, she feels a flicker of pride that Gro Vik took her seriously.

The front door opens and in steps what must be the priest. Nina and Niklas move to one side to let him past, both indicating that he should carry on upstairs.

But why? she whispers eventually. Why *Bluebeard's Castle*?

He looks at her, puzzled, before realising what she's asking.

*Bluebeard* was her favourite folktale.

Her pulse is still racing as she turns off the car engine outside the house and brings her hand to the front door. It's unlocked. When she reaches the top of the stairs she sees Mads sitting at the kitchen table with his laptop and a cup of coffee in front of him.

I'm sure you've heard the news, she says as she enters the kitchen.

What's that? he asks, looking up at her.

Mari Nilsen has been found.

Alive? he says.

No. In the water, just down from her parents' house.

She pulls out a chair and sits down.

What are you saying?

She was washed ashore yesterday. She was found by her parents and her little boy.

My God, he says, covering his mouth with one hand.

She nods gravely.

An accident? he says. Or...?

They can't be sure, she says, picking up her phone. She shows him the article that has just been published online. Bold, white type on a black background at the very top of the page states: 'Missing Woman (30) Found Dead'.

There is a picture of an ambulance with flashing lights and two police cars down by the shoreline in broad daylight. A few police officers stand in conversation at the edge of the photograph, one of them speaking into what she assumes to be a walkie-talkie, if that's even something they still use these days.

The police state that there is no indication of suspicious activity.

Mads is silent, he shakes his head slowly.

And they're quite sure that it's her? he says eventually. When someone's been left for that length of time...

They've identified the body, she reads.

Neither of them utters a word.

That's that, then, she says eventually. Time to focus on the move.

About that, Mads says, getting up. The agent from the house we viewed in Strangehagen has been in touch.

Really? You mean it hasn't sold yet? she asks, surprised.

Oh yes, it sold ages ago. But another interesting prospect has cropped up.

Nina looks at him.

Whereabouts?

In Kalfarlien.

*Kalfarlien*? she repeats with astonishment.

It's not coming to market until the New Year, but I begged them to give us an early viewing. They want us to get in touch.

What are you waiting for? Nina says. Call them!

# Thursday 20<sup>th</sup> December

He stops and turns to face her.

Nice, don't you think? he asks.

Is this it? she asks, speechless.

The large, detached home towers before them.

What did I tell you? Mads says. You just needed to have a little patience. Something was always going to turn up eventually.

Bloody hell, Nina says, it's like a small *palace*.

That might be overstating things a little, Mads says, but they do share certain features, it has to be said.

The agent is leaning against his Tesla on the driveway, waiting for them with an enigmatic smile on his face, keys dangling from his index finger.

Are you ready for this? he asks, walking ahead of Mads and Nina to the entrance, where he unlocks the front door and holds it open for them.

Come on in.

They make their way inside and both instinctively look up before looking at one another.

The ceiling height, they say in unison, and the agent smiles.

Slowly they make their way from one room to the next as the agent comments on various details.

A library, Nina gasps as they enter the next room.

All of the windows in the property were replaced earlier in the year, the agent tells them. Bespoke frames from one of the city's oldest traditional craft workshops.

There's a fireplace in the drawing room, Nina whispers to Mads. I could hold literary salons here.

If only you had any interest in literature. This room is much better suited to gathering everyone involved in a murder mystery, if you ask me.

And a large bathtub, Nina says, sticking her head in the main bathroom door. Surely it's settled on that basis alone?

Have you seen the view out to Ulriken? the agent asks them as they enter the dining room. The sun shines on the veranda late into the evening during the summer months.

Nina sighs.

The kitchen isn't all that modern, but—

That's not important, Nina says, interrupting the agent mid-sentence.

After viewing the house, they step outside and make their way around the corner to the garden.

Look at that, Nina says.

A greenhouse built in the traditional English style, with a wooden framework and brick foundations. She heads straight down the flagstone pathway and opens the door. It smells of black, living earth.

She turns to face Mads.

I'm going to need something to keep me busy once I've had my fill of all this silly literature malarkey, wouldn't you say?

You've always talked about having a greenhouse, Mads says, and she looks at him, inquisitive, is he making fun of her? But he gazes at her with sincerity.

What with you losing the allotment, he clarifies.

She turns back around, gazes at the greenhouse, pictures row upon row of pots, stems abundant with tomatoes, a simple table and a few chairs, and her, sitting there with a book and a herbal tea in her later years.

The agent sticks his head in.

I have to head off, he says. But do get in touch if you have any questions. As I say, they'll be starting all the usual viewings in the New Year.

Do you think there'll be much interest? Nina asks, reluctantly making her way out of the greenhouse.

It's a unique proposition, the agent says, and his words linger in the air. Call me if you've got any questions.

He walks ahead of them in the direction of his car.

Truthfully, Nina says as they stand on the driveway and watch the agent leave. She looks at Mads hopefully, and it takes all her effort not to jump up and down in front of him. What do you think?

I really like it, Mads says.

## Friday 21<sup>st</sup> December

The room is bare and unrecognisable, every sound has a different ring to it; her voice when she speaks to Ingeborg on the phone has a harsh, metallic clang.

She's packed a few boxes and suitcases of essentials to take with them wherever they end up in the New Year. The rest is in storage. They'll probably rent a flat while they wait to move into a new house. Berg tried to persuade the council to cover a week's stay in a hotel, but to no avail.

She stands in her study with a stack of empty cardboard boxes and a roll of bin bags to hand, determined not to take anything with her to her new life that she really ought to have disposed of before now. She's not a sentimental person, so why haul a heap of cold memories along for the ride? she asks herself as she flicks through the stack of papers and folders containing anthologies and reading materials that she's carefully held on to since her days at university, most of which have lain untouched and unread for more than thirty years. She forces herself to dispose of things with conviction.

Before too long the shelves are bare, the drawers empty of papers. The desk is due to be moved into storage with the last car load. She leaves the bin bags in the room; the council have agreed to provide a skip and extra pairs of hands to help clear the house of anything they don't want to keep.

On a decluttering high, she finds her bag and empties the contents onto the floor. Old, crumpled receipts, lipsticks, toothpicks, tissues.

Underneath a pair of leather gloves, Niklas Bull's serious face glares up at her. It's the programme for the *Christmas Oratorio* performance. She picks it up, she hasn't thought about him since she was on Tornøy three days ago. He'd be OK, she'd probably spot him in the springtime with another young violinist by his side. She doesn't harbour any residual guilt.

She lets her gaze wander over the list of performing soloists and halts abruptly.

Mezzo-soprano Marianne Beate Kielland.

It hits her full force, like an electric shock; she jumps.

Anne Kielland, he'd said. That was what Jo had said she was called, the colleague that had tipped him off about a potential tenant.

Her throat tightens, she gasps for air.

He'd lifted it straight from the programme, turning Marianne into Anne.

In a flash she feels cold all over.

Jo, who's achieved great professional success.

Jo, who sometimes acts as if ordinary rules don't apply to him.

Jo, the oncologist.

She is sitting at the dining table in the dark, empty room when Mads comes home. In the soft glow from the lamppost outside, wet fragments fall, melting into the pavement below.

Beside her is a glass and a half-finished bottle. She's spent hours trying to compose herself, but her heart hammers away inside her, she can feel it in her stomach, her chest, her head.

Are you still up? he asks with surprise and stops halfway up the stairs in his black suit and white shirt, his hair damp and ruffled. Nina, he says. What is it?

Sit down, she says, and he climbs the final few stairs up to her, crossing the room with some hesitation before standing before her.

I know you're not going to believe anything I'm about to say. I'm not sure how I'm going to convince you.

He pulls out a chair, sits down.

I'm listening.

She takes a deep breath. Suddenly she doubts everything that she's felt so certain about all evening.

Mari Nilsen fell pregnant when her husband was away. You remember that, don't you?

Yes, Mads says, nodding.

While she was being treated for cancer. And there's good reason to believe that the father...

Is her doctor, Mads says, completing her train of thought. I gathered that. But what makes you think so?

She was obsessed with that phenomenon, transference, precisely because that was what she had experienced. She was attempting to understand herself and what had happened to her, and that's what she found.

I'm not so sure... Mads says. You hear about it from time to time. But a child?

There's more, Nina says.

He looks at her.

I don't expect you to buy this straight away, she says, but hear me out.

He leans back, signalling to her that he's paying close attention.

The colleague that tipped Jo off about Mari Nilsen, she says, the fact that she needed a place to stay.

Yes?

She doesn't exist, Nina says, and Mads furrows his brow.

It was *Jo* who knew her, Jo wanted to find her a place to stay, she continues.

Mads looks as if he's waiting for her to elaborate before his expression quickly changes. He opens his mouth, freezes, then erupts in a brief, dismissive chortle.

Nina, he says. Stop now.

Just hear me out, please. Mari Nilsen had cancer. Jo is an oncologist...

There are hundreds of oncologists working up at Haukeland!

Jo lied to me about it, she says, about his colleague. Why would he feel the need to do that?

Nina! he says, setting his glass down on the table firmly. Seriously.

Nina holds her breath as his expression grows increasingly brooding. He looks at her gravely.

No, he says, his tone firm. He shakes his head resolutely, as if trying to shake the thought itself from his mind. He stands up.

Wait, she says.

It's late. Too late for all this nonsense, he says.

He has a son, Nina says. A son without a mother.

He halts on his way out of the room. He turns around slowly to face her before squeezing his eyes shut, doing all he can to prevent reality from filtering in.

He thumps a finger on the table top, pointing in her direction.

Forget about all of this, he says. He turns around and starts making his way upstairs to the bedroom.

Fine, I'll write to the Board of Health Supervision, she says quickly. They can look into it.

He stops halfway up the stairs.

People have lost their licence for far less, she says.

That's my brother you're talking about.

He turns around slowly.

The girl's dead, he says. What good would it do…? He stops.

She stares at him, open-mouthed.

Do you mean to say…? she begins, trailing off, feeling a tingling sensation spread from her eyes and down her body, all the way out to her fingertips and down to her feet.

She falls silent.

He returns to the table, pulling out a chair and taking a seat.

Hear me out now, Mads says.

I've known since the day we saw a photo of her in the newspaper, Mads says. The day after we got back from Oldervik. Jo rang me.

Nina sits stock-still in the dark room, her heart hammering so hard in her chest that it feels as if the ground is shaking.

He was out of his mind, Mads says quietly without looking at her. He started talking about something that had happened a few years ago. Something that should never have happened at all.

He swallows, his gaze fixed on his hands.

It all just came tumbling out of him, Mads says, the whole story. He'd spoken to her the day before her operation. He knew who she was, obviously, he'd been to several of her concerts.

He looks over towards the window, his face illuminated by the lamppost outside and the light of the overstated advent stars in the windows of the house across the road.

She made a strong impression on him.

Deep lines cross his forehead.

You know what Jo's like, he says. He's so...

Sensitive, she suggests.

Yes. He is. He should never have become a doctor. Not an oncologist, at any rate. He should have gone into plastic surgery or veterinary medicine.

As if they don't see a whole range of fates play out before them, Nina remarks dryly.

He'd been the one to perform her surgery, Mads continues. It had all gone well. That was that.

But then?

Then she'd reappeared in the department a month later for radiotherapy. They got talking. That turned into a coffee, and things changed between them, slowly but surely.

My God, she says. A *patient*.

Things got out of control.

He falls silent. Looks out of the window. Opens his mouth once again.

It all culminated in a night in a hotel together.

A *hotel*?

He nods.

She closes her eyes and shakes her head.

I can't wrap my head around it either, he says.

Was he in love with her?

He falls silent. Takes a deep breath as if to answer her, but stops in his tracks.

Yes, he eventually concedes. But it was short-lived, just a fleeting thing, he knew it was madness. He spoke about her with such genuine warmth and sorrow and fear, Mads says. I think there were a lot of factors at play. They had a lot in common. A passion for music...

Their age... Nina says sarcastically, but Mads' expression gives nothing away.

We'd been renting the place out to a Vietnamese family for a few years, he continues. Do you remember that? Back when Aunt Lena was in the nursing home. But they gave notice around New Year and moved out three months later. Then Jo came along and told me he had a potential tenant in mind, one of his colleague's nieces. He was straightforward about the fact that she was going to be a single mother and needed all the help she could get. She moved in shortly afterwards.

Had she been paying rent? Nina blurted out. Not that it's the most important thing.

Every month without fail. Then Aunt Lena passed away that summer, and I wanted to sell the house. Jo argued against selling it at the time, he said it would be like throwing millions of kroner out the window, that I should hold off. But then he sold his share. I realise now that I should have been more suspicious at the time, he says with a brief, bitter smile.

He asked me to wait, surely I didn't want to kick out a heavily pregnant tenant? You and I had talked about the possibility of Ingeborg returning from Oslo at some point and needing somewhere to live. Perhaps it was just as well continuing to rent it out in the meantime.

And the child is definitely his? she says.

I asked him the same thing. He had no reason to believe otherwise. The boy even looks a bit like him.

And then what happened?

She moved in. I only met her the once, when she collected the keys. She wasn't Mari Bull at that point, so I didn't give it a second thought, didn't recognise her at all. And towards the end of the year she had a baby boy. Jo visited them initially and made sure all was well with them both. He didn't feel any particular joy at the boy's arrival, he had hit rock bottom trying to cope with his lies and double life.

Poor man, she says. She wasn't interested in the three of them living together as a family, then?

I don't think so. Well, perhaps. He tried to avoid the subject, did what he could to phase her out of his life bit by bit. She was kept at arm's length.

And then?

And then you two turned up at her door, it must have triggered something for her. She thought you were Kaia at first, she was terrified, she wanted out immediately. She rang him again and again, he had promised to sort things out, to find something else for them, if she could just stay with her parents for a few days, just to give him a little bit of time.

Nina nods, that lines up with what Sigrid had told her.

Then he spoke to her on the Thursday when she'd been out walking. She sounded different. Unstable. Very upset about an argument she'd had with her mother. Then she started talking about the two of them, demanded that Jo tell Kaia about them and move in with her and their son instead. She couldn't take it anymore; it was too hard on her own. He tried to explain that he couldn't, didn't want to, and then she threatened to expose him, to Kaia, to his employer. Eventually he just told her: do it.

Mads takes a deep breath, looks down at the table.

She started threatening to take her own life.

And?

He begged her to stop, but she carried on, said she was going to do it.

He stops talking.

In the end, he hung up on her.

Nina sits there in silence.

He never heard from her again.

And?

Mads shakes his head.

And nothing. The night passed, and he still hadn't heard anything by the next day. He started to feel anxious, but he didn't make contact. He didn't want to give her false hope. He started to imagine that he might have seen the last of her.

Which was true...

He decided to tell Kaia everything regardless.

To beat Mari to it?

Just to get it out in the open, whatever the consequences.

But?

But when she was reported missing, he decided—

To take stock of things? she suggests sharply.

He's crushed, Mads says, looking up at her.

*He's* crushed? she splutters. Think of her family! Her son! *His* son!

I know, he says, I know, I do.

Not to mention Kaia, she says. The betrayal.

And then when they found her the way they did, Mads says quietly, rubbing a hand over his face.

What happens now? Nina says.

What do you mean? Mads says, looking up at her.

What do we do? We can't just go around knowing about all this and acting as if nothing is amiss.

Mads' face darkens.

I promised Jo, he says, his gaze locked on her. He's so miserable. He knows it'll crush Kaia. He knows her best; he knows how she'll react. Causing more harm now everything's said and done, it's pointless.

How could he do something like this? she asks.

You have to promise me, he says. You can't tell anyone. Not Kaia. No one.

And you've known about it all this time, she says. I've been prancing around like Nancy Drew while you've been playing me all the while, laughing at me behind my back.

Laughing? Mads says. Are you mad? I've been terrified! Terrified for Jo, terrified about how things will work out for him, terrified for Mari Nilsen.

And terrified about what I might find out, she says, her tone steely.

He gives her a long, hard look.

Yes, he says. I've been afraid of that, too.

Are you coming? he calls from the top of the stairs.

She nods feebly.

Soon.

He steps into the bedroom and leaves the door ajar behind him.

It's two o'clock. It's strangely quiet outside. Inside is just as quiet, besides the faint hum of the refrigerator. It strikes her that she ought to sit up at night more often; you miss out on something when you go to bed every night, she thinks to herself.

She refills her glass to the brim as quietly as she can.

She can't seem to slow her heartbeat. Her stomach thuds with it, her throat too, she can hear the rush of it in her ears.

She thinks of Kaia.

How can she possibly not tell her?

How can she know this and not say anything?

Before going to bed he made her swear. Swear never to say a word. It had felt as if they were two children indulging in some sort of solemn game. She doesn't know what it involves, swearing something as a grown adult.

It's as if the news hits her again and again, no less overwhelming each time, everything he told her. It fades and then strikes once again, slamming her over and over in waves.

She opens the lid of her laptop and looks to see if anything further on Mari Nilsen has come to light. Nothing.

She starts clicking through results, browsing a series of images taken at concerts across Europe, numerous old, digitalised local-newspaper articles on the young prodigy, Mari Nilsen, a smiling, gap-toothed eight-year-old, then twelve, sixteen, right up until she conquers Europe under the name Mari Bull, increasingly recognisable as the woman who lived on Birkeveien.

She pictures Jo, perpetually cheerful, permanently unshaven, getting by on his charm and the gift of the gab, impossible to dislike, especially for Kaia. She pictures Jo and Mari as they enter the hotel, making their way past reception together, or perhaps he entered alone.

Later, on Birkeveien. Jo dishing up lies for his brother, playing down the scope of things, she knows that from the diary. Jo, with promise after lie after promise after lie, keeping her warm, keeping her at arm's length, asking her to be patient, telling her they'd be together before long, the two of them, or the three of them to be more accurate, Mari would just have to wait that little bit longer.

Nina closes her eyes and tries to shake the image from her mind.

Promises and lies, until eventually she can take no more and ends everything.

She opens up German websites and sees older interviews automatically translated into a staccato, outlandish version of Norwegian. Mari Nilsen talks about her upbringing, her enthusiastic parents who unearthed her talent, sacrificing aspects of their own careers to lay the groundwork for her life, remarking on the fact that she was never pressured into practising, that it was always something she did with passion, always.

Suddenly it hits her: the willpower required to drown oneself, to step out into the water and simply forge ahead, Virginia Woolf with her pockets filled with rocks, or to take a great leap out into the black water, to feel it fill your mouth, too salty, enter your nostrils, your stomach, your lungs, submerged, struggling and rising to the surface once again, then back under, then up for air. The last thing you see before sinking for the very last time is the light in the window of the housing estate where you grew up, way off in the distance. Behind one of those bright spots of light, your son lies in bed, sleeping peacefully.

Perhaps it's the same willpower that one requires to practise five hours a day as a child, she thinks to herself. She slams the lid of the laptop closed.

She knocks back her glass and fills it once again.

Nobody can know. She already knows too much, she wishes she could erase it all from her mind, live in blissful ignorance, she should never have started asking questions. She can never talk to Sigrid or Toralf Nilsen again, never look them in the eye, mustn't ever run into them. She'll never be able to relax in Oldervik again.

She feels the faintest hint of sympathy she'd had for Jo during the talk of his anxious weeks slowly dissolve into nothing, then transform into aggression. It is as if reality begins to filter in: taking advantage of a patient in his superior role as a doctor. A terrified patient, a demigod in a white coat.

Jo is just the tip of the iceberg. You read about it, she thinks, complaints of sexual assault against doctors. But the thought of all those incidents that go unreported, the people allowed to simply carry on doing what they do. Because patients feel guilt. She knows she would. A willing victim.

She pours herself another half-glass, the bottle is empty. She pictures his face, his lupine sneer, his dishevelled hair, the man who gets away with everything. How many others had there been? she wonders. She recalls what Kaia said – it's never just the one.

She takes one deep breath after the next, can't seem to calm herself down, thinks of Kaia, wonders what the right thing to do might be, she has no idea.

Her phone is in her briefcase. She could call the police right now.

She tries to imagine what would happen if she really did make contact with Gro Vik, if she were to lay bare all that she knows. She is instantly filled with doubt, is this a police matter, is the investigation even still ongoing, now that Mari Nilsen has been found? What would the police do with information about the identity of the boy's father? It was still a suicide, after all.

She opens her laptop once again.

Pulls up the Norwegian Board of Health Supervision website.

She looks around for a moment before finding the search box, then types 'complaint'.

A series of results appear, and she quickly locates the right link before clicking on it.

She skims the page, the blocks of text a grey mishmash before her, and eventually she finds the section aimed at patients who wish to make a complaint, or next of kin who wish to lodge a complaint on behalf of a patient. The advice is to contact the county commissioner.

She lifts her glass. Kaia. How would she take it? Nina is conflicted: she wants to hold back and yet she feels the desire to push ahead. Kaia, she thinks to herself, she deserves to know. To know what kind of man she's married to, no matter how painful that realisation might be for her. She has to know. Nina would want to know.

She places her glass down hard on the table and searches for the county commissioner website.

She selects her region and is immediately faced with an error message. She tries again and is sent to another empty webpage.

She feels a sense of relief, but also a sinking sensation. The regional reform everyone's been rolling their eyes about for months is blocking her way. Stopping her attempts at justice.

All of a sudden, she pictures little Ask and his grandparents in the house on the estate, despondent, deprived of answers to any of their questions. Blaming themselves and each other for not having stepped in earlier, for not having read or understood the signs, for having left their daughter to sail her own sea.

She goes back to the home page and types 'county commissioner complaint patient' and is redirected to the correct form.

It's just a case of entering the information.

She lifts her glass to her lips and knocks back the contents before placing it down and starting to type, tapping the keys softly, silently.

She quickly and concisely outlines the situation, the relationship that developed between the doctor and patient in question, the child that was born, relevant dates, all outlined simply and matter-of-factly.

Her finger is shaking as she presses 'send'.

The pain in her stomach almost causes her to lurch forwards and is quickly followed by overwhelming nausea.

An error message pops up: such-and-such a field hasn't been filled in correctly. She quickly glances at the page, identifying the issue and correcting it before submitting the form once again.

Another error message: page cannot be loaded.

She clicks refresh and everything disappears without warning, everything she's written, all of it, gone.

Everything seems to collapse around her, she sighs heavily. She lets her head fall back.

She closes the lid of the laptop just as the bedroom door opens and Mads sticks his head out.

Are you coming?

I'm coming.

She stands up. Her knees are quaking, relief: she doesn't need to do it. Nothing will happen if she just leaves things be, no catastrophe will be unleashed, no lives will be destroyed.

Everything can carry on as it was.

## Saturday 22nd December

They eat breakfast in silence the following morning. They've finished their last few days at work, and now the holiday has started and the final few boxes need to be packed up and driven to the storage unit. Each of them takes a floor of the house, making their way through the rooms systematically, the place unrecognisable by the time they've taped up the last few boxes, an empty shell.

What do you make of it? Mads asks as they survey the unfamiliar upstairs. The final few brown boxes have been stacked up by the front door.

She starts to cry, quite spontaneously, she hadn't seen it coming, she feels the pressing sensation behind her eyes, her face crumples.

There, there, he says, wrapping a reassuring arm around her.

It's not that, she hiccups quietly.

I know, he whispers. I know.

Her phone rings as Mads carries the boxes out to the van, it's Kaia. She doesn't answer, it rings again, she doesn't answer.

Mads comes in after a short while, covering the phone with his hand and mouthing Kaia's name, she's checking whether they're coming for Christmas Eve or not. Nina shakes her head firmly. Mads lifts the phone to his ear and explains that they've decided to spend Christmas in Oldervik.

I don't think I'll be able to speak to them normally ever again, Nina says as Mads hangs up.

She sinks down onto the stairs, he sits on the step below hers, stroking her ankle.

Give it time, he says.

She looks up at him, red-eyed.

The fact that you've known about this for so long... she says, and her voice breaks.

He stares blankly into the distance with his arms resting on his knees.

That's almost the worst part.

I'm so sorry, he says. I've been on the verge of telling you so many times.

She thinks about how close she came to reporting her brother-in-law and shudders at the thought.

He's my brother, Mads says eventually.

Kaia is my best friend, she says. How can I carry on knowing this and acting as if nothing is wrong?

But what good would it do... Mads begins. Who would it benefit? Certainly not Kaia. Not Jo. Mari's family won't get their daughter or mother back.

She is silent.

We can be certain that he won't do anything like this again. He's already paid the price. He's been like a cat on a hot tin roof for the past four years.

He buries his head in his hands and breathes deeply. They have to move on.

Maybe we should do it? she says, looking up at him. Drive to Oldervik, after we've stopped by the storage unit?

He looks at her with surprise.

Pick up some nice food and spend a few days there by ourselves?

Mads gets up, picking up the final box.

# Christmas Day

Work on the project proposal on representations of the self in the age of the algorithm is progressing slowly. She feels strangely enthusiastic, relieved to have returned to normality.

Over the past three days they've taken long walks after breakfast, strolling through the impressive park down by the college and onwards, along the small, frosty gravel paths that weave their way through the huge trees down to the shore. They've spent long, silent mealtimes together. Worked. Sat at their desks reading, writing, drinking coffee. Mads has cancelled everything he had scheduled between Christmas and New Year.

The beginnings of her neglected students' assignments have been read and scrutinised; she's prepared long, detailed feedback that she is looking forward to conveying after Christmas. She feels somewhat abreast of things for the first time in a month.

They celebrated Christmas Eve very modestly with a few aquavits by the fire, each reading through their own stack of documents interrupted only by the creak of the cast-iron wood burner.

She sits at her desk and looks out of the window. It's a clear day, the sky an acidic shade of yellowish-grey, the fjord beneath it shimmering like liquid mercury.

She goes through her briefcase to find her diary and finds herself pulling out a small, black notebook instead, and she feels her stomach lurch; she is struck with the immediate desire to toss the book into the fire, to watch it go up in smoke. Why had she put it there in the first place? she asks herself. Perhaps so she could have *something* of Mari Nilsen's, she hasn't got anything else.

She is overcome with the need to rid herself of it.

Still feeling reluctant, she opens the slim notebook filled with its characteristic, sloping handwriting.

Slowly she leafs through its pages, there's a different rendezvous on Birkeveien almost every day of the week. A combination of unease and excitement spreads through her when the scale of the situation hits her. It burns inside her, this is what he's been up to, visiting her, visiting his son. He'd told Mads that he'd barely seen her after making sure that all was well after the birth.

She opens her laptop and searches the terms she doesn't understand.

The entries, all dated, range from spirited to deeply depressed, up and down, week after week, from January to the beginning of November this year. She's optimistic, waiting for Jo to leave Kaia, then *lamentoso* in the next second, mournful, *con brio*, with vigour, or *con fuoco*, fiery, and frequently *amoroso*, followed by *sospirando*, sighing, *ziehen* and *zögernd,* it's dragging on, she's unsure.

Nina squirms, all these visits, and with her son around? And he got away with it. Kaia blissfully unaware, blissfully humiliated.

Gradually there is more *amoroso*, more *scherzoso*, playful, interspersed with the odd *doloroso*, melancholy, and *pesante*, heavy.

It's a textbook example of how to string someone along, close and warm one day, distant and cold the next, endless switches between optimism, doubt and utter heartbreak, she can't end things with him, or rather: he won't *let* her end things with him. An iron grip.

And on the final page: *Morendo*. That was how she felt, like she was dying, dwindling, her life over.

She closes the book, lays it down.

## Boxing Day

She wakes with a sense of peace, a cold, clear stillness. Something about the light is different. She gets up, makes her way over to the window. A soft, white lid conceals everything beneath it.

Mads has already set the table for breakfast by the time she makes it to the kitchen.

They hear the snowplough approaching, but otherwise all is still.

After eating, she gets up and heads off to continue working. Mari Nilsen's notebook is still sitting on her office desk. It strikes her that it might offer some comfort for her parents that their daughter's mood was prone to such dramatic shifts, it was clearly beyond their control, they couldn't have done anything differently.

In the suitcase in the porch, she sees her gift for Milja sticking out of a plastic carrier bag. They hadn't managed to see Ingeborg and Eirik before they'd left for his parents' house.

If it's true that children use fairy tales to work through trauma, then there's someone who would be better off with the book than Milja.

She sticks both the notebook and the gift in her bag.

Mads is on the phone in the dining room, chatting as he paces the room in circles.

She steps into the hallway and pulls on her thick parka, then slips her feet into her winter boots and finds a hat.

Eventually she takes a deep breath and pushes open the door.

The world outside is still and white.

The snow glistens, soft, completely flat besides a few small bird tracks.

She starts tottering uphill, stepping between the soft, quilt-like mounds of icy crystals beneath the clear, blue sky above.

The fjord twinkles silently as she reaches the top of the hill. There is no one to be seen, not a car in sight, she crosses the road and wades through the snow in the direction of the housing estate.

She hears Sigrid's footsteps on the stairs as the sound of the doorbell reverberates through the house.

Do let me know if I'm disturbing you, Nina says as the door opens.

Sigrid shakes her head, steps to one side.

Come in, she says.

Nina kicks the toes of her boots against the steps and manages to shake off most of the snow before following Sigrid inside. Ask is lying on his stomach and gazes at her between two stairs.

The living room is filled with flowers, huge bouquets in vases covering every table, cupboard and desk.

A little something for you, Nina says, passing him the wrapped gift.

Present, he says, his eyes wide. She crouches down beside him.

Would you like me to help you unwrap it? she asks, and he nods gravely.

She pulls at the tape and helps him to unwrap the book.

Oh, Sigrid says feebly. Look at that, Ask.

*The Complete Fairy Tales of Charles Perrault*, Nina says, looking at Sigrid. Mari's favourite is at the end. But it might be an idea to keep that one for further down the line.

The little boy starts flicking through the beautiful illustrations with excitement.

What do you say? his grandmother says.

Thank you, Ask says very seriously, his eyes fixed on the pictures.

Little Red Riding Hood, he says, holding the book up to show his grandmother.

I've got something for you, too, Nina says, sticking a hand inside her bag and passing Sigrid the notebook.

What is it?

I'm sorry, Nina says. It's Mari's. It must have fallen out of the box.

Sigrid turns the notebook over before opening it up.

Quickly she browses through it, her gaze flitting up and down over each page.

But this isn't Mari's, she says.

What?

Where did you find it?

It was with her other notebooks, Nina says.

Her other notebooks? What notebooks?

The ones in the box, Nina says. The box I brought you.

There weren't any notebooks in that box, Sigrid says.

There were two. Plus this one.

No, Sigrid says, there weren't... she shakes her head, perplexed, she seems irritated.

Nina grows irritated herself at the fact Sigrid doesn't seem to believe her.

See for yourself, she says. She takes the book, opens the first page and holds it up. It's a diary.

This isn't Mari's diary, Sigrid maintains, she looks away.

She's noted down her state of mind...

That's Toralf's handwriting, Sigrid says.

She looks at Nina.

That's his diary.

Nina leafs through the pages as she continues to hold the book up for Sigrid.

But, she says, it's ... he's ... there are hundreds of entries, in this one and the others, it says Birkeveien after every date entered.

He used to visit her quite often, Sigrid says with a brief shrug. I was working, but he was retired.

She stares at Nina. Her gaze is piercing.

He's a real mother hen, you know, Sigrid says with a brief, nauseating smile. He helped her out a great deal.

Nina does her best to grasp what Sigrid is telling her, her head is spinning, she tries to catch her breath.

*Amoroso*, she mumbles, *con brio*, she riffles through the pages of the notebook. *Con fuoco*? Sigrid looks at her, puzzled.

Grandma, look, Ask says, holding the book up for her to see.

*Morendo*, Nina whispers.

The wolf, he says with fear and delight, looking up at them expectantly with his grandfather's dark-brown eyes.

Where is he now? Nina asks, her voice low.

Sigrid grows hazy in front of her, Nina's hands start to shake, she tries to take deep breaths, wants to stop the trembling, but it is as if her throat is closing up.

Sigrid gives her an odd look, what is it? she asks, Nina waves a hand.

Nothing, she says hoarsely with a faint smile.

She stands up quickly, too quickly, she's unsteady, dizzy, she supports herself with a hand on the back of the sofa.

What is it? Sigrid asks again, scrutinising her.

Nina takes a few unsteady steps towards the staircase, her gaze wanders over Ask in the reading nook, captivated by the fairy tales. She grasps the bannister at the top of the stairs.

She remembers it now.

What the police said, that people don't tend to surface very far from where they drowned.

Sigrid gets up and comes after her.

Are you leaving? she asks, surprised.

Nina focuses on her breathing, she mustn't fall, can't fall down the stairs, mustn't lose her footing, it's slippery, she's wearing her woolly socks, she sees Sigrid approach.

It was you, Nina whispers, can't tell if she's said it out loud or just thought it to herself. Toralf, she thinks, Toralf and Mari, but the thought remains incomplete, she sees Sigrid furrow her brow and stop directly in front of her, she looks inquisitively at Nina.

She hurries downstairs, holds on tight, but Sigrid follows her.

Nina, she can hear behind her, right behind her, and in front of her the door opens and there he stands, blocking her way.

Nina, Sigrid repeats behind her, you've gone pale, and Nina is trapped there between them, her eyes prickling, white spots rolling in front of her like a pulsating mass, there's a crackling in her ears, and then she hears nothing, everything goes black.

She is woken by the gradual return of sound around her, the rushing in her ears growing fainter, the spots dissipating. She sees an unfamiliar ceiling, lights sting her eyes, she sees her legs hovering in front of her, high up, she can hear fast-paced footsteps on the stairs. A tall, slim figure appears in front of her, growing clearer with every moment that passes, there he stands, staring at her, she stares back.

There you are, he says, and she sees the contours of his face as they gain clarity, until she eventually finds herself gazing at the eyes behind the spectacles, the white, close-cropped beard.

Hurry, she hears him say, and she sees Sigrid appear on the left with something shiny in her hands.

She wants to get up, but her feet, they're nowhere near solid ground, she stares at them with terror.

Drink this, Sigrid says, handing her a glass.

You fainted, Toralf says, carefully lowering her legs.

Sigrid places a hand on her back as she helps her up, she sits up on the warm tile floor, brings the glass to her lips and takes a sip, follows their instructions.

What happened? Sigrid asks. You wanted to leave all of a sudden?

Nina remembers, she remembers the episode in the living room, Sigrid, the notebook, Mari's diary, not Mari's diary, but Toralf's?

I... she begins, looking at them. They look back at her with a combination of concern and curiosity. She can't say anything. She has to get away.

She gets to her feet, brushing herself down lightly with her fingertips. She looks for her shoes, there they are, and there's her coat too, in the hallway, she needs to get to it.

Wait, Sigrid says, we can't send you out there alone, not with how slippery it is, not after fainting like that.

I'll go with her, Toralf says.

She tries to piece things together, to guide everything she knows into place, the diaries in the box of Mari's things, three diaries packed with entries, all written in code, a language that Toralf and Mari shared?

The fact that it hadn't ever occurred to her before now, the young prodigy and her proud father, the pair of them travelling here and there and everywhere together since childhood, always close, so close, and exactly how much did Sigrid know and understand of that? Was she aware of it? Was that why she had been so angry at her daughter? What was it that he was describing in his diaries, all of his visits, all of those occasions he'd travelled to Bergen to be with her? Only to then give them to her in order that she could read about his feelings, was that how he controlled her?

Nina steps back, away from him.

Grandad? a feeble little voice says. They turn around. Ask peeps through the stairs once more. Grandad, I've got a book, he says. Come and see.

Wait there, Ask, Toralf says. We've got a visitor.

I'm leaving, Nina says, she takes a step towards the door.

I'm afraid I have to insist on coming with you, Toralf says, grasping her upper arm and locking eyes with her.

So that's why she moved to Bergen, Nina thinks to herself. To get away from her father.

Sigrid turns away and makes for the stairs, just as she always has, looking the other way.

Get your things on, Toralf says. Nina pushes her hands through the sleeves of her thick coat and sticks her feet in her winter boots. It's broad daylight, she thinks to herself, there are neighbours, he can't do anything. But when they step out into the snow, she's struck by just how quiet it is, so blindingly white and so very quiet, every sound stifled, she could shout at the top of her lungs and she couldn't be sure that anyone would hear her, the snow covers the landscape like a blanket.

I'll drive you, Toralf says as they stand on the front steps, I've just cleared the snow off the road.

I'd rather walk, she says stiffly. The fresh air will do me good.

You're quite sure? he says.

She thinks that she ought to call Mads, she has to warn him, he can come and pick her up before Toralf takes her away in his car and drives her somewhere nobody would think to look. She rifles through her pockets but in that moment she sees it, her mobile phone lying on the kitchen worktop by the radio back in the cabin.

Was that what he did, Nina thinks to herself, put his daughter in the car and drove her somewhere ... drove her down to the jetty, threw her in or forced her to jump? But why?

Toralf looks at her inquisitively.

Jealousy, she thinks to herself. He found out about Jo.

Rage at having been betrayed.

And Ask. Whose son was Ask?

She turns towards the house, at the big window upstairs she can see Sigrid, standing there watching, looking down on them with a tense expression, as if she'd rather look away but can't bring herself to do so.

What are you going to do to me? she blurts.

What do you mean? he asks, giving her a strange look.

She knows she's out of luck, if he wants to grab her now then he can, she wouldn't be able to get away.

Why did you do it? she asks, and her voice sounds faraway, as if it isn't her saying the words.

What are you talking about? Do what?

She starts down the path, away from him, but he comes after her.

Do what? he repeats.

She carries on walking, he follows her, she walks faster, he matches her pace. Do what? She looks for cars, people, someone to call out to, but there's no one. It is as if every house is snowed in, there's nobody to be seen, and she's jogging now, but Toralf appears by her side.

Do *what*? he asks again, this time through clenched teeth. She squeezes her eyes tight shut as he grabs her arm, holds her back.

What is it you think I've *done*? he asks, and he looks at her, wide-eyed, taking shallow breaths, tiny puffs of frosty air firing out of him, shooting in her direction. She says nothing, she wants to open her mouth and roar but knows that no sound will emerge.

It's not what you think.

Nina says nothing.

I realised there was a notebook missing, he says. In the box you brought over.

Nina pulls away, she starts walking again, they're out of the housing estate now, she crosses the road and makes for the gravel path leading to Oldervik, wonders what he'd managed to do to her before they had made it this far.

I know it looks odd, those notebooks, he says. From an outside perspective.

Nina walks, eyes ahead of her, woodland on one side, water on the other, she wades through her own tracks in the snow, just a short kilometre, then their cabin will be in her sights. He's still coming after her, doesn't let her gain more than a few feet before catching up.

It was something I started doing as a music student, he continues. A kind of logbook, it's a habit that's stuck with me. And when Mari fell ill … Ill, then pregnant, then divorced. Then she gave up music. Mari was strong, but everyone has a breaking point. I was afraid she was getting there. A single parent without a foothold. I visited her often. More and more frequently after Ask was born.

Nina listens, stares straight ahead, concentrating on walking, just walking.

She had a mild case of antenatal depression, she had doubts about her abilities as a mother. I started taking notes after my visits, just to keep track of how things were going. A few brief words about her and Ask, what things were like between them. It was a little bit up and down. But they were so good together, Toralf says.

I gave the notebooks to her when we were there for his third birthday. To show her how well things were going, to reassure her that she didn't need to have any doubts, I'd made notes after every single visit. The love between her and Ask, it—

She hears his voice crack and make way for a powerful sob, she slows down, sees him out of the corner of her eye, his face contorted.

They were the most perfect pair.

She turns to face him; his expression is bleak with sorrow.

I'd never have believed that she could ever... he says, his lips quivering.

He shakes his head.

Never, he repeats.

Nina stops. They're in Oldervik. Her cabin is just around the corner.

But, she says, *come prima*? What—

Like the first time, he nods. She'd been so happy just after he was born. Before depression sank its claws into her.

*Morendo*?

The depression, he says. It had disappeared, died. That was my assessment, anyway. How wrong I was...

I'm sorry, Nina says quietly. She looks down at first, then meets his gaze, but she looks away once again, she feels ashamed.

She says nothing.

She knows he's telling the truth.

They say... he begins. They say it's not unusual. For perfectionists. That she felt she'd failed, believed that Sigrid and I were disappointed in her.

Who says that?

The police. Failing to live up to expectations, constantly attempting to improve upon one's accomplishments, right up until it's no longer possible. Eventually there's only one way out.

They stand ankle-deep in snow, the forest all around them, utterly silent, neither of them speaking a word.

He shakes his head.

She doesn't know what to say.

I need to get back, Toralf says eventually. There's a lot to do before Friday.

Friday?

Yes, he nods, the funeral.

I'm so sorry, she mumbles. Their eyes meet, briefly, before Toralf turns around and makes his way back, a stooped figure making his way through the snow.

She steps inside, kicks off her boots, heads into the living room and collapses into a deep armchair. She closes her eyes, hears Mads' slippers on the floor.

The door opens.

He looks at her as if he's seen a ghost, phone in hand.

Mads, she says feebly.

The house, he says, almost breathless. It's ours.

What?

We got it.

What are you talking about?

Mads is open-mouthed. He seems stunned, slowly sinking down in a chair of his own.

You called them today, on Boxing Day?! she cries.

I had a feeling... he says, staring into space. The agent dropped a few hints. The vendors, they needed a quick sale.

She stands up.

And it was true, he says.

How much? she asks.

Don't you worry about that, he says gravely, before the corners of his mouth curl upwards in a smile.

He gazes at her, a devil-may-care expression beneath his cool and collected smile.

Amazing, she murmurs. He gets up, wraps an arm around her and holds her close. Amazing, she repeats, burying her face in his neck, feeling the fizz of excitement fill her chest.

How shall we celebrate?

With family, Mads says. Let's invite them here, all of them.

Ingeborg's lot?

Ingeborg's lot, he says, plus Kaia and—

She pushes away from him slightly, shaking her head.

No.

Nina, he says. The sooner you see him, the better. Otherwise things will only snowball.

She falls silent.

Nina, don't you agree this is worth celebrating?

Of course, she says. Call them.

# Thursday 27th December

Ingeborg, Eirik and Milja arrive early afternoon the following day. Every last trace of snow has been washed away by the rain that fell overnight. They head down to the water's edge and throw pebbles in, all of them together, but turn back when clouds darken the skies above, even though it's still early in the day.

Before they've made it indoors, a gale begins to whip around them. Mads jogs home with Milja on his shoulders for the last stretch as she wails and howls in jest at every buffet of wind that chases them.

By the time they make it to the house, Kaia and Jo's car is already parked up outside.

Through the kitchen window she sees her sister-in-law measuring out coffee grounds. A shiver runs through her, she wriggles her shoulders and takes a deep breath, opens the front door, jumps in.

Got the old countryside uniform on, I see, Nina remarks breezily, nodding at the wool jumper that Kaia never otherwise wears, and the fancy-looking shawl around her shoulders.

Merry Christmas to you too, Kaia says.

Where's Jo?

In the living room.

Nina sticks her head through the door, unperturbed, he's on the sofa scrolling on his mobile.

Merry Christmas, she shouts through to him, and he glances up, ready to stand up and greet her. No need to get up, she says, slightly too earnestly. She's made up her mind to keep her grudge well buried, it's like Mads says, what good would it do, what good would anything do now? But still she can't bear the thought of embracing him.

He opens his mouth to speak.

Your phone's ringing, Kaia calls through from the kitchen.

She turns around, relieved, her phone is vibrating on the kitchen worktop. She doesn't recognise the number, but answers all the same.

A young woman introduces herself but Nina doesn't catch her name; she responds absent-mindedly as she runs a cloth under warm water.

The woman apologises for disturbing her, but hopes that it might be a convenient time to talk. I've run into an issue I think you might be able to help me with.

You have?

I was just processing your complaint, the woman begins, and Nina stops her abruptly.

Who did you say you were?

I'm a case officer for the county commissioner's office, the voice replies.

The county commissioner? Nina repeats, and Kaia turns to look at her with surprise.

That's right, the woman says.

Nina turns off the tap, she feels as if she's on the verge of blacking out again, leans against the kitchen worktop for support.

I'm calling about your complaint, the voice says.

I see, Nina says, quickly leaving the kitchen and making her way into the bedroom, fumbling her way along the walls for support.

So the form had been submitted after all.

She collapses onto the bed.

I can't see anything to suggest that the doctor you mention treated the patient in question, the voice asserts.

No, Nina says quickly, it's an error, I made a mistake. Please ignore my whole complaint.

Really? the young voice says. Are you sure?

Quite sure, she says. I apologise if I've caused any inconvenience.

No need to apologise, the woman says. I'll delete the complaint. Goodbye.

She gasps for air. Her hand trembles as she places her phone on the table in front of her. She focuses on her breathing until she slowly regains the feeling in her body. My God, she thinks to herself, bringing her hands to her mouth. My God, what an idiot, what a complete and utter fool.

So close.

She takes a deep breath, remains seated until she can feel the blood circulating around her body normally, waits until it's safe to get up. She goes down to Kaia.

What's up? Kaia asks as Nina re-enters the kitchen.

What do you mean? she replies abruptly, and Kaia looks at her with surprise. Nina hastily begins arranging various Christmas biscuits on a plate.

It's all about to kick off, I think, Kaia says.

What?

The storm, she says, gazing out of the kitchen window. Listen.

They hear a faint rumbling sound outside, the tree trunks creak.

Did you see the newspaper on Christmas Eve? Kaia asks as she pours the freshly brewed coffee into a pot.

No, Nina says, why do you ask?

You remember that awful Me Too consultant we talked about a while back?

The one staff had warned management about?

That's the one, she says, taking the mugs from the cupboard. She's been given the sack.

Is that so?

Jo dealt with it, Kaia says proudly.

Nothing quite like a scapegoat, Nina thinks to herself, taking the biscuits through to the living room, where the others are sitting around the fire, listening to the increasingly tempestuous gusts of wind with concerned expressions. She avoids making eye contact with Jo.

I saw that she's been found, Kaia continues impassively as Nina returns to the kitchen to fetch the coffee pot.

Who? Nina asks, but then she realises who Kaia means.

So, it was suicide, then?

An accident, suicide or something in between the two, Nina replies. She was washed ashore a few hundred metres from here.

Pfft, Kaia says. At least it's winter.

What do you mean?

A body immersed for a long period in water warm enough to bathe in? That wouldn't be a pretty sight. Birds and fish would have gone to town on her.

True enough, Nina hisses through clenched teeth, and Kaia gazes at her, perplexed.

Nina feels a swell of rage at Kaia's casual references to Mari Nilsen's death when it was *her* husband who was so much to blame for the outcome.

I'm just saying. Ice-cold salt water isn't the worst thing a person could end up immersed in.

Nina inhales deeply to keep herself from making any further remarks.

Do you happen to know if they've done a psychological autopsy? Kaia asks, clinking and clattering the dinner plates.

A what now?

A psychological autopsy, she repeats. Interviewing the family members left behind, assessing her mental health to decide the most likely cause of death?

No, but how would I know? Nina says, trying her best to sound neutral.

You're in touch with her family, aren't you? People think that mental-health issues are to blame for nine out of ten suicides, Kaia says. But that's not the case.

Really?

Those left behind find it easier to blame a psychiatric diagnosis than to accept that someone has decided to desert them, and so they posthumously assign one to the person in question. Chronic depression, and so on and so forth.

I see, Nina says flatly.

But suicide is often a carefully considered act executed by a psychologically healthy individual. Many of those who take their own lives have a realistic view of what the future holds for them and make a decision based on that: is this a future that I'd choose for myself? Actually, no.

Nina ties up the bin bag and places it on the floor in the hallway.

She fits the profile, Kaia reflects as Nina returns.

What profile?

Many of those who take their own lives are perfectionists. Successful people who've developed an identity from early on in their lives that is both extremely delicate and highly performance-based, one that makes them vulnerable, even when it comes to minor setbacks. She was a child prodigy, wasn't she?

That's right, Nina confirms.

And she suffered some setback or other as an adult, fell away from music?

She nods.

She felt like a failure, like she'd disappointed her parents. She felt as if she'd been rejected. She hadn't managed to live up to the ideal intended for her. Life hadn't gone to plan. Previously her strategy had been to consistently improve upon her performance, but when that no longer worked, suicide offered her a way out, Kaia says, reeling off her explanation of events in the same way the police had done for Toralf.

But it's years since she gave up music, Nina says. For the past few years, she's...

She's what?

She's been a single mother, Nina says briefly. She falls silent.

Kaia stops and turns to face her; Nina is afraid she'll hear her heart hammering in her chest.

I think it must have been an accident, Nina says, her sister-in-law's eyes on her.

It's easier to tell with men, Kaia says briskly. If their fly is open then it was an accident, but if not? Suicide.

Eirik reads aloud from his phone that the next ferry has been cancelled due to the poor weather conditions.

Lucky we got here at the time we did, Kaia says. Where's Mads gone?

He's speaking to the city council's duty officer, Nina says.

The power's gone out in Bergen, Eirik says, continuing to read aloud in a monotone voice, as if he's a breaking-news app they've installed on the sofa.

Oh God, the freezer, Jo says with concern, looking over at Kaia.

Whereabouts in Bergen? Nina asks.

Møllendal, Kronstad, Fløen, your side of town, mostly, Eirik says.

Bloody hell, Nina says, grabbing her phone to send a message to their neighbour, who has a set of keys for the house.

Ingeborg clears her throat and looks at her inquisitively.

Your freezer is at the second-hand shop, remember?

Oh, of course.

These New Year storms, Jo says, they never fail to catch me by surprise.

Mads returns from the kitchen.

Do you have to go in? Nina asks.

Not as things stand, Mads says, they've got it covered.

He and Jo grab their oilskins and head outside to see if anything has come loose that might need securing in place.

The rain alternates between battering the windows and hammering on the roof, coming in sudden, powerful gusts. Through the kitchen window she sees the two of them deep in conversation under the shelter of the woodshed, Jo throwing his arms out, Mads lifting his palms to halt his gesticulating. She assumes that Mads is letting him in on what she knows, but that she's promised not to say anything. By the time they've come back inside and removed their wet clothes, both seem to have calmed down.

A few times that evening, she catches Jo's anguished glances in her direction when he thinks she's not looking, but she gives nothing away.

Eventually she calls everyone to the table, they all get up and find their places. She places the lobster gratin on the table as Mads pops open a bottle of champagne. The heat from the wood burner beams in their direction, the wind howling outside.

Welcome, everyone, Nina says, raising her glass once Mads has poured some champagne for them all, plus sparkling water for Ingeborg.

We're so glad you could all make it at such short notice. It was touch and go, she says with a nod in Kaia and Jo's direction. They smile and raise their glasses.

Milja pushes her chair out from the table abruptly and hops down onto the floor, where she finds her iPad. Ingeborg helps her to open up a game, and a discussion ensues between Eirik and Ingeborg about whether Milja should be allowed to have the sound on or not.

Nina stands there, her glass still raised.

We've got something to celebrate, she continues, with a discreet smile in Mads' direction.

The others exchange surprised glances. Jo glances at her nervously, as if Nina might say anything in that moment.

Ingeborg, Eirik, she says, tilting her glass in their direction. Congratulations on your early inheritance.

They lift their glasses and exchange broad grins.

Milja, she says, nodding at the floor. A new nursery. Good luck! The recipient of the toast shows no sign of having registered the warm words intended for her.

Kaia, Nina says. Finally, a lady in command!

Kaia laughs and clinks her glass gently against Jo's.

Jo, Nina says, swallowing. Out of the corner of her eye she registers Mads watching her, expectant.

I understand that you've made a positive start in your new job by cleaning house, she says, and he smiles nervously.

Clearly the right man for the job. Congratulations.

The others raise their glasses in Jo's direction, he gives a brief, grateful bow to Nina, then holds her gaze a tad longer than usual.

And Mads, she says eventually.

The others turn to Mads with curiosity as he smiles at her mysteriously.

Mr Patient, she says with a sigh. Patient to the point of coldbloodedness! We've spent thirty-five wonderful years together on Fløenbakken, she says, and he nods.

The thought of saying our final farewell to our home in just a few short days only to make way for a long queue of machines ready to turn the place into kindling... She trails off, and has to swallow.

I have to confess that one of us has found that harder to accept than the other, she says, clearing her throat. But you. You've taken it all in your stride, just as you do with everything. Perhaps that's the reason I, a young student with a passion for the classics, fell for you, a stoic medical student.

Mads gazes at her fondly.

Stoicism is one thing, she says, *sophrosyne* something else altogether, and she registers Ingeborg rolling her eyes at Eirik inconspicuously.

Remind us what that means again... Kaia says.

Wisdom, temperance, calmness. *That* was the deciding factor, Nina says, and Mads accepts sarcastically reverent bows from everyone around the table.

We're inching towards my area of expertise, Nina says, continuing her speech, which some among you may have heard I was unfortunate enough to badmouth very publicly.

The others exchange glances, laughing with some uncertainty.

I can assure you all that I no longer harbour dreams of becoming an investigator, Nina says, and Kaia bursts into laughter.

That's something, her sister-in-law says. You're a fine example of why literary scholars ought *not* to join the police force. You'd have had them chasing one highbrow, intellectual lead after the next when the obvious answer was right in front of your nose the whole time.

Nina feels her frustration grow at her sister-in-law's boldness, but keeps her cool. She takes a deep breath and looks at her family.

She's happy to be moving on, happy to reconcile herself to the realities, to pack them up and put them away, to discard them, just as she's discarded so many things from her life in the past few weeks.

A few weeks ago, I lectured my students on Greek tragedy, she continues, in which the concept of *hamartia* plays a central role.

Meaning? Ingeborg interjects.

Error, Nina says. An error in one's evaluation of a situation, brought about by the tragic hero's limited powers of judgement.

Her gaze is involuntarily drawn towards Jo, who immediately stares into his glass.

Hamartia mustn't be confused with hubris, arrogance. Accidents do not occur as a result of moral flaws or guilt on the part of the character, nor due to a failure of character; they are quite simply the result of a fatal mistake, she says.

Kaia and Mads look up at her with interest as Jo continues to gaze downwards.

To err is human, Nina says. We often stumble in the dark, unaware of the full scope of our actions.

Ingeborg and Eirik exchange vaguely condescending looks.

The fact that my own husband had to partake in the decision to tear down my childhood home is a perfect example of what we would call tragic irony, Nina continues, uncertain how to get her short speech back on track, and Mads nods.

But unlike the Greek tragedies, instead we here see a sudden shift from bad luck to good, she says, raising her glass in Mads' direction.

You'll be lord of the manor over in Kalfarlien in the New Year.

The others wake up, staring at her in disbelief.

*Kalfarlien?* Ingeborg says, slack-jawed. Seriously?

Kaia looks from Jo to Mads to Nina with bewilderment.

Cheers! Nina says, lifting her glass above everyone's heads.

The others join her in a toast, and Mads gets up, kissing her briefly on the mouth and hugging her tightly.

Now: dig in! she says, sitting down.

At that very moment, pitch-black darkness envelops them, as dark inside as it is out, besides the glow of two candles in the middle of the dining table and the blue light of Milja's iPad, which illuminates her on the floor like a little ghost.

Eirik instinctively reaches for his phone and turns on the torch.

Mads, there are candles in the top drawer in the kitchen, Nina says, making her way over to the mantelpiece on the hunt for matches. Kaia grabs a few candlesticks from the china cabinet while Jo goes outside and returns with another bottle of champagne, which he opens with a pop.

In the confusion, Nina gets up and walks through the kitchen and into her bedroom. She sits on the bed, drops her head to her knees and sobs twice, silently. Then she sits upright, takes a slow, deep breath and stares directly ahead of her. The reverberations from her sobs transform into an odd chuckle. She laughs involuntarily, perched on the edge of the bed, silent, shaking, intense, before all is once again still. Then she gets up, clears her throat and returns to the others.

In her absence, uproar has gripped the living room.

Milja's iPad has run out of battery.

She's inconsolable; Ingeborg and Eirik, both exasperated, do their best to calm her down, but nothing will do. They try chocolate, biscuits, offer to let her play something else on their phones, reassuring her all the while that the power will be back before too long, but the little girl simply screams and screams as she writhes around like a snake, doing the best she can to bang her own head against the table.

Kaia and Jo observe the situation with strained, slightly disdainful expressions, as childless people tend to whenever they witness parents helplessly kneeling before their offspring. Mads begins helping himself to the food.

Nina is gripped with a rush of frustration at the sight of the two parents mollycoddling their young child and swiftly strides across the room, grabbing Milja under her arms, hoisting her up and saying: Time for a spooky fairy tale with Grandma!

Her granddaughter doesn't stop howling, but Nina carries on regardless, carrying her through the house and to the bedroom, where she pulls off Milja's tights and Christmas dress as she thrashes around, then she tucks her up under the duvet of the double bed.

Once upon a time there were two children named Hansel and Gretel, Nina begins.

No! Milja shrieks.

They stumbled across a witch who wanted to cook them up in her giant cauldron, she reels off without hesitation.

*The Hares and the Frogs*, Milja says firmly.

What was that?

*The Hares and the Frogs*! Milja barks.

Do you remember that one? her grandmother says with astonishment.

*That one*, Milja says, and Nina crawls beneath the duvet beside her with satisfaction and begins regaling her with the requested fable.

The Hares were having such a terrible time that they decided to take their own lives, Nina begins, and with that, the tiny body beside her releases every ounce of tension and Milja curls up under the covers and listens intently.

By the time Nina has finished telling the story of the hares who opt against their collective suicide plan, encouraged by the idea that others are having a worse time of things, Milja stares at her expectantly with newfound respect, and emboldened by her granddaughter's curiosity, Nina launches into an ad lib rendition of the tale of the fox and the stork.

No! Milja growls bluntly. The lion and the fox!

The lion and the fox?

The one with the lion in the cave, Milja replies.

Oh yes, *The Sick Lion*, yes, Nina says. Let me see. She scans her memory for the story: The old lion, King of the Beasts, had fallen ill. He lay in his cave, groaning and sighing, unable to move a muscle. The other animals weren't sure what to do, but decided to console him with a visit. All creatures great and small visit the King – all but the fox. When the lion finds out, he sends the jackal to ask why the fox hasn't been to see him, she says, remembering then that she hadn't ever read the fable to the end.

Then what? Milja asks.

I'll tell you the rest if you close your eyes, Nina says.

Milja closes her eyes obediently and Nina discreetly grabs her phone from the bedside table and hastily looks up the fable online.

Aaaand ... the fox replied, she says, scrolling down the list of hits until she finally finds the one she's looking for.

'And the fox replied: It's not that I don't wish to see our king. Quite the contrary! I value him as highly as everyone else. Several times now I've been on my way to see him, always with a little chicken bone as a gift—

'Yes, but then what happened? the Jackal asked impatiently.

'Well, then I spotted something that frightened me, something that stopped me in my tracks, in spite of how keen I was to pay the king a visit. I saw a great number of animal tracks in the sand outside the lion's cave, trails left by all manner of creatures great and small, but all of those trails led *inside* – straight into the mouth of the cave. I couldn't see any tracks leading back out the way. And that caused me to reflect upon the matter, the fox said. And that was that.'

Milja opens her eyes wide and Nina quickly places her phone back down where she'd found it.

But why? Milja asks.

Why what?

Why? she repeats.

Why didn't the fox go into the cave, you mean?

Yes.

Because the animal tracks only went one way: *into* the cave, Nina says.

But why? Milja asks.

Because the animals never came out again.

But why?

Because the lion gobbled them up.

Why?

Because it made for a much more relaxing hunt, her grandmother tells her. Instead of having to run around the savannah on the lookout for something to eat, he had all the animals come to him. It was much easier that way.

Milja thinks hard for a moment.

So, the animals are inside the cave?

They're inside the lion's tummy, Nina says.

In the cave?

Yes, inside the lion's tummy, which is inside the cave, she says.

She strokes Milja's forehead, running her finger from her forehead down to the tip of her nose, and Milja's eyes immediately grow heavy. She's developed magical powers where children are concerned, she thinks to herself as she lies there stroking and stroking and stroking her granddaughter's face, until Milja lets her head drop back onto the pillow, closes her eyes and finally breathes heavily.

She lies by her granddaughter's side for a while, staring at knots in the wood of the ceiling planks, just as she used to do in the house on Fløenbakken as a child; she discovers contorted faces gnashing like animals, with pointed noses like snouts.

She thinks about the story of the sick lion, she's quite clever, really. Milja got it in the end. The tracks all lead into the cave.

She wakes with a jump to see the ceiling light flashing. The power is back on.

She leaps out of bed and over to the wall, where she hits the light switch to prevent Milja from waking. She glances at the clock, how long has she been here? No more than twenty minutes, she sees.

The door opens slowly and Mads pokes his head in cautiously.

She brings a finger to her lips and he nods in acknowledgement with his eyebrows raised as he spots the sleeping child in the middle of their bed.

She creeps out of the room, silently closing the door behind her. He wraps an arm around her.

Not bad.

Oh, you know how it is, she says. Sometimes Grandma knows best.

She accepts a standing ovation from the other guests in the living room for her unrivalled child-wrangling expertise.

Tell us, how did you manage it? Kaia asks.

I simply put my subject area into practice, she says. The world's oldest profession.

Isn't that... Eirik begins.

No, she says authoritatively. The world's oldest profession is *storytelling*.

OK, says Ingeborg, so that speech you gave before about tragedy and the power of judgement and all that, it was a bit... and she pulls a face and opens and closes her hand like a blathering mouth. Everybody knows that the main reason literature exists is to scare children into keeping their mouths shut and staying in line. That, and putting them to sleep. But let's be honest, that's pretty vital!

Isn't that so! Nina says, enthused by her daughter's long-awaited recognition, and she allows her glass to be filled with golden bubbles.

# Friday 28<sup>th</sup> December

The rain pelts the car. Slowly they drive up the gentle slope in the direction of the college. Ingeborg is scrolling on her phone in the passenger seat, googling recipes for baked trout, while Nina asks her to add item after item to the shopping list.

How are you feeling? Nina asks.

Ingeborg cocks her head to one side.

Not bad, she says. Tired.

The atmosphere had improved as the previous evening had gone on. She'd managed to relax. She took care not to drink too much, afraid of what she might say to Kaia. She let the others do the talking and was the first adult in bed, cuddling up next to Milja.

She is still struck by a shiver that runs through her whole body at the thought of the call she received from the case officer at the county commissioner's office, how close it was.

Maybe it's like Mads says. He's had his punishment. Four years of unease, that's quite enough.

At the crossing by the college they have to stop to let a hearse pass, heading in the direction of Bergen. She catches the merest glimpse of a white coffin, and she gives a start. Was it today? she thinks to herself slowly, has to count the days. Friday, that's right, it *is* today, it might be her in there. It had completely slipped her mind. She'd been thinking of attending, but then their visitors arrived, and then...

More than anything she wants to spin the car around or take a different route; the car sits motionless at the crossing.

Hello! her daughter says. Drive.

She hits the accelerator and joins the stream of traffic making for the heart of Tornøy, past the housing estate, slowly and inescapably approaching the church as the windscreen wipers struggle against the onslaught of water.

The square outside is swamped in black, people on their way towards their cars in search of cover from the sudden, intense showers.

She has to stop in order to let a group of people clad in black cross the road in front of her, just beyond her bumper they hurry on their way with umbrellas turned inside out, making for the car park on the other side of the road.

But isn't that… Ingeborg says, staring unabashed at the crowd of people outside the church.

Nina catches a glimpse of Niklas Bull, standing alone, looking mournful in a drenched black coat, his dark curls wet. He stands at the foot of the steps leading into the church, gazing vacantly into the distance.

Yes, she says, that's him. She wants to drive on, but more people want to cross. The rain hammers down in the light of her head-lamps. The windscreen wipers zip from side to side at full tilt.

And… Ingeborg says, then falls silent.

Nina sees the same thing, the elderly couple in the middle of the car park, one of them with a child in his arms.

The crowd around them is breaking up, they huddle close to one another as the man does what he can to protect the child from the rain with his coat.

There they stand, the three of them alone, heavy with grief, with guilt, as everyone around them flees the awful weather. They've just watched the car pull away and drive north, towards the cre-matorium in Bergen. A daughter, a mother, inside a coffin.

Yes, Nina says, that's them.

She glances briefly at Ingeborg and is surprised to see her daughter blinking away a tear.

A car behind her beeps its horn, she jumps and hits the accel-erator, the tiny family in the car park becomes smaller and smaller in her rear-view mirror.

She lays the trout on the worktop, dill and fennel seeds, garlic, lemon, butter. Looks out. A sudden shift to blue skies. The others are changing into their walking gear, preparing to climb the most child-friendly of the local peaks.

She thinks of Kaia, Jo, the ticking time bomb between them that might split wide open and shatter everything at any given moment. It all depends on how cold he is, how good he is at suppressing things, at justifying them. He's obviously taken great pains to cover his tracks, the case officer couldn't find his name and he referred her to another doctor when things started heading in the wrong direction.

She chops herbs, her gaze fixed on the lawn outside, then jumps as the blade slips and slices through the nail of her index finger. She places the knife down.

She feels a sense of unease that refuses to leave her.

As she watches the group disappear into the distance, head to toe in outdoor gear as they make their way around the bend in the road, she digs out her phone.

She looks through her call log and finds the number she's looking for before tapping on it, nervous as she hears a click and the sound of a throat being cleared. The voice at the other end belongs to a woman on the switchboard, Nina realises after a moment of confusion. She introduces herself and explains in the simplest terms she can that she was called by a young female case officer the previous day but that she can't recall her name, and would it be possible to find out who it was, if she happens to be there?

The woman on the switchboard utters a brief, hoarse chortle, as if the thought alone is far-fetched, but asks her to hold for a moment.

As silence emanates from the receiver, she opens the lid of her laptop and types 'salivary gland cancer' in the search field. She places her mobile on speakerphone and sets the phone on the table, scrolling down the list of results.

Yes, hello? a voice says, unexpectedly breaking the silence, and Nina jumps as she grabs the phone.

Are you the person I spoke to yesterday? she says. My name is Nina Wisløff.

Yes, that's me, the woman on the other end says, and Nina recognises her voice. What can I help you with?

I asked you to delete a complaint, Nina says.

Yes, that's right.

Is it possible to reverse that, by any chance?

Unfortunately not, the woman says. You'd have to submit a new complaint.

She feels her heart sink.

But you mentioned that the doctor in question hadn't been treating the patient, she says.

Silence falls at the end of the line, a silence that Nina hopes is rooted in a sense of doubt on the part of the case officer.

I *could* take a quick look at my notes, the woman reluctantly concedes after a short pause, yes I have them just here. One moment, please.

Nina's gaze wanders over to her laptop, and she clicks on an Oslo University Hospital link about the treatment of salivary-gland cancer. She skims the text on the page. If the individual's condition is like so, the treatment is like so, and so on and so forth. For a growth located beneath the chin, treatment would involve an operation, then a six-week course of radiotherapy, the same treatment Mari had undergone, followed by regular check-ups, every other month initially, then every third month after that, all of which were to be conducted in the ear, nose and throat department.

She freezes. At that precise moment, the case officer pipes up.

This is a little imprudent, the woman says, but OK. There was talk of a doctor by the name of Glaser. But his name wasn't Jo.

Thank you, Nina whispers, and she clutches the phone to her chest.

She pictures her face clearly. The way she stiffened in the doorway in front of them as Ingeborg introduced herself as Glaser.

Hello, the voice at the end of the phone says. Nina ends the call.

She can sense him standing behind her.

What is it? he asks. You look like you've seen a dead body.

She turns to face him.

I thought you'd gone out with the others? she says.

I had a phone call I needed to take.

He sits down opposite her.

Who was that on the phone? he asks breezily.

Cold caller.

He glances at the screen, raises an eyebrow.

What are you reading up on now, then, eh? he asks cheerfully.

You were her doctor, she whispers.

What? he says.

It was you...

He looks at her, open-mouthed, his face frozen with a cheerful, quizzical smile on his lips.

Ask, she says, then has to gasp for air. Is he *yours*?

His expression changes.

What are you saying?

He must be, of course he must, she mutters under her breath. She feels everything beginning to break away, tiny pebbles at first, each of them disappearing and making way for larger rocks, breaking and smashing against one another on their way down, down, down, until eventually the biggest boulders start to shift, toppling, tumbling, until everything has come crashing down around her.

Nina, he says. What's this about?

She sees him grow pale. His expression darkens.

Her head in her hands, she presses her fingertips hard along her brow ridge, squeezing her eyes tight shut.

Everything you told me about Jo. It was you all along.

I'm so sorry, he says finally, without looking at her.

Four years? she says, looking up at him. How could you do it, all this time?

He remains silent.

And then to lay the blame at your brother's door, she says, unable to look at him. What kind of person are you?

But I stayed with you, he says eventually. Even though she wanted...

She bursts into bitter laughter.

Oh, thanks! she splutters. I'm sure that had nothing to do with the fact you'd have lost your job if it had all come out? You'd have lost your medical licence!

He looks down.

It was always out of the question, he says eventually. It's always been you, always will be.

He lets out a sob that rings hollow.

Cut it out, she snarls. She brings her hands to her head, feels the ground beneath her feet shifting, rotating in waves, the nausea rising up from within her.

What happened? she whispers.

I don't know, Nina. I don't know.

How did it happen?

He looks up, shaking his head.

She turned up to receive her diagnosis alone, he says. There were seven of us, seven doctors and nurses facing her there, all alone at that first meeting when she received the news. She was so small, all by herself, white with fear.

And then? Nina says.

We had a brief conversation the following week, the day before her operation. She was alone then, too. I performed surgery on her, it all went well. I looked in on her briefly the following day, and that was that.

And then?

She started seeking me out. Over and over again. At work, long after her operation, while she was having radiotherapy, when I no longer had any part to play in her treatment. She'd sit in the corridor waiting for me to pass by. Just to say hello.

She looks at him.

Or in the canteen, he says. As if by chance. It happened on numerous occasions, she turned up all over the place, just to see me, or for me to see her.

He takes a deep breath.

On one occasion she stopped me, trembling with nerves, telling me she was convinced the cancer had spread. I don't know if it was just a pretext or if … it seemed genuine. I needed to calm her down. She had so many questions, and nobody had the time to answer her.

And?

We started talking. I was on a break. I tried steering her onto a different track, she was locked on to the idea, she sensed the disease everywhere. I told her we'd seen her perform at Grieg Hall. Brahms. I asked if she'd been able to practise at all, if she had her violin there with her. She was just looking over sheet music, she said. The radiation field, he says, bringing a hand to the left side of his throat, it was exactly where her violin sat, it had started to hurt.

He falls silent.

And then, she says.

It all repeated itself. She would appear. We would talk. Her appetite for human contact was insatiable.

Insatiable, she says, mimicking him in a whisper.

One evening I'd been working late and was on my way home when I bumped into her at the top of Fløenbakken. She told me she was taking a walk, but I knew.

She'd found out where we lived.

God knows how long she'd been standing there, he says, pacing back and forth, up and down.

And you invited her in.

He swallows.

Into our home.

He closes his eyes.

What were you thinking?

He shakes his head, he doesn't know.

A *patient*?

She was going to be OK, he objects, and she laughs, flabbergasted by what he considers to be an apology.

So what happened?

I told her it could never happen again. I realised that it had to be some sort of reaction, some sign that I needed a break. That was a good while before the election. I told the party that I was ready to take on a role, if that was something they'd be willing to consider.

You already knew she was pregnant by that point.

Yes, he nods. She told me in the spring, during her first check-up, the nurse had left the room for a moment. I was aghast – I'm sure you can imagine. She needed help, she was getting divorced, moving out. She asked me to help find her somewhere in Bergen.

And what exactly did she have in mind?

As I said, he says. She hoped we might ... but I made it very clear that was out of the question.

And?

And so she moved into the house on Birkeveien. We had minimal contact, she lived there rent-free, obviously, but otherwise she got by on her own.

And then?

Then the boy arrived. He ... I visited them when they got home from the hospital.

Who was with her for the birth?

She was alone.

And? she says, feeling a lurching sensation in her chest.

And nothing, he says. I felt nothing. Only remorse. Remorse and unease.

Don't lie to me, she says with a hiccup.

It's true. There was nothing there. I knew she thought that everything would change when I saw him, that we'd be a family. But all I wanted was to come home. To forget everything.

Forget everything, she repeats.

After that, I saw them as infrequently as possible. The odd practical job around the house would crop up every now and then, which I always took care of, but we never had…

She waits.

A relationship, he says eventually. After that, I mean.

He looks up at her.

It's the truth.

And then you went around for the next three years acting like nothing was amiss, she says.

It was easier than I had imagined it would be, he says with a bleak smile. All I wanted was to forget about it, forget that it had ever happened, just to be with you and Milja, to focus on my work.

It very nearly worked, she whispers.

You should never have mentioned the house to Ingeborg, he says quietly. Mari became…

So it's *our* fault, Nina says sharply, and he turns around.

No, obviously not. God no.

He's silent.

But she had only just begun to accept the reality of the situation, he says. She was there. She had a child, a job, she was happy with her life, she was in the process of reuniting with her ex-husband. And then you two turned up and shook the foundations.

She stares at him in disbelief.

You blame me, she says, her voice shaking.

No…!

Can you hear yourself?

I'm just saying everything was fine, it was all going well. Then, out of the blue, I get a hysterical phone call.

What did you do?

She just wanted out. I helped her, she didn't have many possessions, I moved them to a storage unit for her, it wasn't a big job. Then I asked her to go to her parents' and take things easy.

And then?

That was that.

She shakes her head.

No, she says. You spoke to her on that Thursday.

It was just a brief encounter.

Encounter? she says.

He looks at her quizzically.

You had that conference at Solstrand...

He falls silent, slowly reddening.

She gazes out into thin air; everything starts to hit home.

You met her here.

She was hysterical, he says firmly. I had to calm her down.

You talk about her as if she's a child, she says quietly, a child that needs calming down.

She threatened all sorts, he says. Threatened to tell people everything, to take her life if I didn't...

If you didn't do what?

What?

She was going to tell people everything if you didn't do *what*?

She wanted me to leave you, he says.

So there *was* a relationship, she says slowly.

No...

She can't help but laugh at the lies flowing forth without end, at how helpless he is.

What have you done? she whispers suddenly, turning to face him.

He looks at her, a strange expression on his face, his eyes transparent, his gaze hollow.

The realisation dawns on her slowly.

She'd never have taken her life anywhere there was a risk she'd be discovered by her parents, or her son, for that matter.

All of the tracks end here.

Her lungs, she says, and her voice doesn't sound like her own.

They never checked her lungs.

Nina, he says, faraway now.

You took a bath, she says slowly. Like you always do, like you always want to.

Nina.

Everything was fine. You had some wine. But then she started up all over again. Demanded you leave me, threatened to expose you...

No, he whispers.

It's bathwater, not seawater. Isn't it? In her lungs, in her stomach.

She sees him shaking his head.

And then you dressed her, she says, her voice distant.

Dressing a wet, limp body. That can't have been easy, can it? Driving her down to the jetty just in front of her parents' house, heaving her up there and dropping her in? You knew they'd had an argument, a fragile artist, it was always possible that she'd take that step.

Are you mad? Mads says, reaching a hand out towards her, as if to stop her.

I could call the police right now, she says.

He looks at her, terrified.

She hasn't been cremated yet, she says. What with the power cut yesterday, the bodies must be piling up at Møllendal Crematorium.

Slowly he becomes clearer, looming in front of her, his expression changing.

In a few hours, this will all be over, he says coolly. She'll be gone, nothing but dust, and you can forget it all. Everything can carry on as it always has.

She gets up.

Don't go, he says, and he stands up too, raising a hand. She steps back, scared, he's well built, he'd easily overpower her, they're all alone, he could do it all over again.

He looks at her, aghast.

Nina! he says. I could never do anything to *you*... He reaches a hand out towards her.

The same hand that had held her head underwater.

It's like you said yesterday, he says. What did you call it? *Hamartia*?

She nods slowly.

A miscalculation? A result of our limited powers of judgement? Mads...

It isn't about morals or blame, that's what you said. Just a tragic error. You know me. I'm not a bad person, am I?

She says nothing.

To err is human, isn't that what they say? We have no concept of the full scope of our actions.

Slowly she shakes her head.

You can decide, he says. Me in prison, the house gone; you could paper the walls of your bedsit with the double-page spreads all about you. Living alone, wallowing in malice, your family splintered, Ingeborg, Milja – all those lives ruined.

He walks towards her.

Ingeborg, he says. She's only in her first trimester. A shock like this could...

He stops.

What's the point? he says. When we could just let things go?

She tries to think her way through the options, to gain some kind of oversight. If he were to turn himself in, perhaps he'd receive a shorter sentence. She couldn't be dragged into things, she hadn't known anything about it, he'd acted alone...

She takes one step after another, moving back before stopping in the corner by the old stove.

I know how good you are at adapting to things, he says. It's just a case of telling yourself the right version of events.

Her legs can no longer bear her weight and she collapses in a heap in the corner.

Do you really think it's better that her family thinks she was...? He stops. Do you think they'd find any comfort in that?

They think it's all their fault, she rasps. They think they drove her to it.

He says nothing.

She sits on the wooden floor, motionless, heavy.

Everything has been shattered to pieces.

She sees it all floating past her as she remains immobile, feeling her body sink further and further down. She can't help but picture her, there in the bathtub, naked, underwater, face down, her hair like a dark, heavy blanket over the back of her head, arms flailing to begin with, then limp, eyes bulging.

She doesn't want to see it, she squeezes her eyes tight shut, doesn't want to see it, would rather gouge out her own eyes than see that.

He sinks down beside her.

Just think what I was willing to do, he whispers, to keep us together, us. This. I know how wrong that sounds, but still, think about it.

She feels a faint tremble spread throughout her body.

Soon we'll be in our new house, he whispers, stroking her knee. You know how much we've been looking forward to it. A new start, he says.

Who knows about any of this? she whispers.

Nobody, he says.

Jo? she repeats through her tears.

Nothing.

He lied about who found us a tenant, she says, looking at him.

I asked him to do that, Mads says. He doesn't know what it's about. You can be sure of that.

No witnesses? she asks slowly. Nobody who's seen anything they don't understand, only for it to fall into place for them at a later date?

Nobody, he says.

What if they were to find something on her phone...?

He shakes his head.

She had another phone, he says. Unregistered.

Where did you learn all this? she mumbles.

She gets up slowly, makes her way over to the window and keeps her eyes on the road. The others could be back any minute, they've been gone a long while now.

She turns to face him.

Can you live with this? she asks him.

I can, he replies after a moment. He looks at her, a grave expression on his face.

Silence falls between them; she can hear nothing but the sound of his breathing.

Can you? he asks, hesitant.

She says nothing.

He comes up behind her.

I know what I'm asking of you, he whispers, his lips brushing her hair.

She brings a hand to her mouth to conceal a sob.

I don't think I can bear it, she whispers, shaking.

We'll help each other through it, he says. He turns her around and looks at her, taking her head in his hands and holding her still, their gazes locked on to one another.

I know you can do it, he says.

She frees herself and makes for the sink, splashing her cheeks with cold water. She wets a cloth and wipes the kitchen table.

Are you OK? he asks, and she nods, taking a deep breath.

She clears her throat, relaxes her shoulders.

Mads fills the coffee pot with fresh water and measures out ground coffee. She stands on her tiptoes and pulls out the tins before arranging an assortment of festive cakes and biscuits on a plate.

Here they are, he says, his eyes on the road. Eirik appears around the bend with Milja on his shoulders. Jo and Kaia are just behind them, walking hand in hand.

She dabs at her eyes with her fingertips and finds a jug for orange squash.

Actually, what about some hot chocolate? she says, looking over at Mads.

Yes, he says, smiling, Milja would love that.

She takes the milk from the fridge, cocoa powder, sugar, bends down and finds a pan. She concentrates on taking slow, deep breaths, tries to compose herself, slowly, slowly.

Have you seen that car before? Mads asks, nodding in the direction of the window. She joins him by the window. Kaia and Jo, and Eirik with Milja on his shoulders, all step to one side, letting a car pass them as it rolls onwards in the direction of their front yard.

No, Nina says, finding a whisk.

Strange, Mads says. He lifts a hand and waves at Milja through the window; she waves back from where she sits on her father's shoulders.

As Nina whisks cocoa powder with sugar and a little water until the powder breaks up and the mixture starts to bubble, another car appears further down the road.

Where's Ingeborg? she asks, nodding at the four of them outside. She opens the door into the hallway.

Her walking boots are there on the hallway floor, untouched.

Mads... she says slowly.

The first car stops in the front yard, its doors swinging open.

Behind the second car, a third now appears, all three with tinted windows. Jo and Kaia stand in the ditch by the side of the road and observe the passing convoy with surprise.

Mads? she repeats. He looks at her, the paper-thin cabin walls. She crosses the kitchen and opens the door leading to the guest bedroom.

Ingeborg is sitting on the bed. She gazes straight ahead of her, phone in hand, trembling.

❧